THE SHILL

JOHN SHEPPHIRD

THE SHILL

A Tale of Deception

Down & Out Books
3959 Van Dyke Rd, Ste. 265
Lutz, FL 33558
www.DownAndOutBooks.com

Cover art by Roger Huyssen
Cover layout by Ricardo Netro

ISBN: 1937495981
ISBN-13: 978-1-937495-98-5

For Jennifer

CHAPTER 1

Work as an actress was sparse. Jane survived by a variety of dead-end, part-time jobs. This one, working for a private investigator, paid minimum wage.

Six months ago, on a foggy morning in L.A.'s beach community of Playa Del Rey, she sat in her Nissan waiting for the subject to emerge from his apartment. Her task was to videotape the man as proof he was physically mobile without the assistance of a wheelchair or crutches. Jane worked for Tim Peduga, an ex-cop turned PI who specialized in insurance fraud.

She arrived just before dawn and found a spot across the street from the apartment. She parked in front of a modern house under construction and hoped the contractors, when they arrived, wouldn't make her move. She could hear the rumble of jets from adjacent LAX airport in the distance.

Jane checked herself in the rearview mirror and hated what she saw. There were bags under her eyes, her forehead was breaking out and her chin looked puffy. Thirty years of age and these moments of self-doubt came more and more often now—a deep, dark depression knocking at the door.

Neighbors walked dogs past. A FedEx truck stopped down the street. She fought boredom by listening to celebrity podcasts on her iPod.

Finally the man emerged from his apartment. It was definitely the same guy from the photo she'd been given. He had shoulder-length curly black hair parted down the middle and a long, scraggly beard. She thought the only thing missing was a flowing black cloak and he could pass for Rasputin, the famed Russian mystic.

She powered the camera.

Even though the video was time stamped, she was instructed to shoot the front page of the *L.A. Times* first. Her boss Tim explained that a video time-stamp could be manipulated after the fact but a physical newspaper is undisputable proof. She supported the lens on the steering wheel and zoomed in.

Rasputin unlocked the door of a Toyota pickup and searched the cab before emerging with a pack of cigarettes. He smacked the pack of Marlboros on his palm and peeled back the cellophane, tossing the remnants into the wind. He produced a lighter and lit the smoke.

That's when he noticed her.

She averted her gaze, pretended to be busy with something below the dash while still keeping the camera trained. In the LCD viewfinder she saw him walk toward her. She dropped the camera and went for the ignition. The car sputtered and stalled.

He was closing in fast.

She locked the doors.

"Excuse me," he said angry. "What are you doing? Do I know you?"

She averted his gaze and tried to start the car again. No luck. *Piece of...*

He tossed the cigarette at her windshield and smacked the hood. "Were you filming me? You don't have the right!"

She pumped the gas as the starter whined but the Nissan would not fire. *Damn it!*

"Give me the camera, bitch!"

What'd he call me?

Jane defiantly flipped him off. She regretted it when it only enraged him more.

Red-faced, he ran around the car and rummaged through the pile of construction refuse. He came back with a cinderblock raised over his head.

You've got to be kidding.

Jane ducked below the dash just before the windshield shattered. Chunks of broken glass rained down into her hair.

Over the cinderblock on her dented hood she could see him searching for something else to throw. She went for the ignition again. The car finally started with a mighty roar.

His eyes registered fear.

"Motherfucker!" she screamed. She threw it into drive and punched the gas.

Boom!

Rasputin flipped over the hood followed by the sound of his head hitting the pavement—much like a watermelon cracking open upon impact.

CHAPTER 2

Months later, dressed in frayed clown regalia, Jane performed a magic trick under the shade of a gnarled ficus tree. For the audience of children she held out an over-sized "die," the singular term for dice she made clear to the kids, and placed it in a black lacquer miniature cabinet. She closed the two doors and tilted the box to one side before she opened the adjacent chamber.

"See, it vanished."

She shut that door and tilted the box the other way—the children hearing a *thunk* as the die seemingly slid to the other half of the box. Opening the opposite door Jane said, "All gone. Show's over. Thank you very much."

The kids screamed in protest. They demanded she open both doors at the same time but she pretended not to understand them. When they had been teased enough, Jane opened them both. The die had disappeared.

"Not everything is as it appears," she said.

This was the final line of her magic routine. She reached into a nearby hat and pulled out the die as if it invisibly jumped through space.

Jaws dropped in amazement. It was her best trick, Jane's grand finale, an over-the-counter magic shop standard hailed "the sucker die box"—no sleight of hand required and the art of deception at her fingertips.

Later, as the rambunctious kids ate ice cream outside French doors, Jane packed her show away. Kneeling on a thick Persian rug in the master bedroom she paused to gaze at the antique four-post bed, its fine linen, silk pillows and a pure white duvet ironed to perfection. God, it must be nice to be this rich, to wake up in a bed like this. For a brief moment she could daydream until—

"That was great." The woman of the house was there with purse in hand. "Thank you *so* much. Brady and his friends loved your act."

Here was a woman who has everything, this tasteful house, a six-year-old boy, a family of her own. She was the lucky one who woke up every morning in this wonderful bed—obviously with a man who loved her. And worst of all, she appeared to be only a few years older.

"Two hundred dollars, right?" the woman said.

Jane nodded and continued to pack her show away. She felt deep envy, the feeling creeping up into her throat, copper to taste, bitter. She needed a drink of water but did not feel like asking. When she finally stood the woman handed her a check.

"I thought we agreed on cash," Jane said.

"I didn't have a chance to get to the bank. I can call my husband and have him drop by the ATM, but he won't be back until later."

Jane bit her lip. She *needed* cash. She could not wait for the stupid husband because she'd be late for class. Jane thanked the woman and took the check without glancing at the total.

Standing in the driveway, still dressed as a clown, Jane waited for her taxi.

She dug out her last thirty dollars and hoped it would be enough to get across town. Once there, she knew she could bum a ride home. This sleepy, tree-lined neighborhood north of Montana Avenue in Santa Monica was once dominated by single-story, pre-war craftsman bungalows. Jane could see that most had been torn down and replaced with two-story, imported-tile McMansions. She found the check to take a look.

No tip. *Figures.*

Jane wondered why the wealthiest people tipped the worst, or, as in this case, not at all. She hated having to rely on taxis but her car was in the shop again, this time a "broken timing belt," whatever that was. She'd nicknamed her car rusty-yet-trusty Nissan, but now it was held for ransom by Yuri her mechanic for six hundred dollars plus storage charges since he'd had it so long.

Not long ago she was working for Peduga Investigations when the crazy Rasputin smashed her car's windshield. Tim paid to replace the glass, plus a little more, and now Jane had nothing to show for it. She suspected Tim wasn't calling her for surveillance gigs anymore because of that incident.

Being a private investigator seemed flexible enough to allow for her acting pursuits, and Jane figured she could eventually hang her own shingle when she became a licensed PI. She'd done the homework and was collecting paystubs as proof for the required hours needed to get her license.

Then last month, just after the Nissan got out of the body shop, it betrayed her. She'd had to tow it to Yuri's and the tow alone cost her a hundred and twenty bucks.

But this job, two hundred dollars, would not liberate the Nissan. The money would go towards food, overdue rent and piles of laundry. She would revive her spent pay-as-you-go cell phone, and maybe tackle one or two of the minimum payments from the stack of final notices collecting dust. She checked her watch again. Where was that damn taxi?

Twenty minutes later, in the back of the cab, she peeled off the silly costume. Jane could feel the Arab's eyes in the rearview mirror.

"Can you hurry, please? I'm going to be late."

"I drive fast-as-can, lady. Don't want speeding ticket."

With a towel Jane wiped the clown-white off her face. She caught him peering again. She was used to men looking at her, ever since she was a teenager— eyes lingering, drinking her in.

She tried her best to ignore the cabbie, slipped on a white blouse and then removed her athletic bra underneath, a learned maneuver from doing quick-changes backstage in school plays. She stuffed her clown costume into her bag and finally dug out her sides, the script pages with her lines.

On the way to acting class, in clogged Los Angeles traffic, Jane studied her lines.

* * *

By the time the meter neared thirty dollars Jane still had more than a mile to go. She told the cabbie to pull over, handed him all the money and apologized for the lack of tip. She could sense his disappointment but there was nothing she could do.

Lugging her suitcase full of magic tricks, wearing a simple white blouse and wrinkled black linen slacks, Jane walked to class, sweating from the heat.

The shabby theater strip on Santa Monica Boulevard, lined with tiny ninety-nine seat theaters, was Hollywood's equivalent to New York's Off-Off Broadway. Under a marquee for Brecht's "The Good Woman of Setzuan" she rushed past a strung-out prostitute. Upon closer inspection Jane saw the hooker was actually a guy in drag, quite normal for this part of town.

The class had already begun, and Jane tried to slip in unnoticed. No luck. Jeremy Sands, her acting coach whose guidance supposedly had steered a well-known student to an Oscar years ago, stopped mid-lecture.

"Well, look who's late again," he said.

The group of acting students seated in the first few rows eyed Jane.

"I'm sorry, Jeremy."

"What's that on your face?"

"What?"

"That..." he said waving his crooked finger at her, "that hideous white stuff, darling. On your face!" Jane ran her sleeve across her forehead, a hint of residual clown white smearing off.

"I...uhm. I do birthday parties," Jane said quietly.

"I beg your pardon," he said with flamboyance.

"I was working. As a clown."

"A clown?"

"Sorry I'm late."

She noticed a new student in the class, an attractive man in a black turtleneck standing in the shadows. He was staring at her. Jane felt two feet tall.

"Everyone else seemed to make it here on time," Jeremy pointed out. "Face it, Jane, you're always late. Are you going to be late to the audition of your life?"

Jane said nothing, anger burning. She suspected Jeremy was mad because she was months behind in tuition. She remained silent, eyes downcast. She focused on the chipped paint in the concrete floor.

Jeremy let it hang there for an uncomfortable beat. "We hope not," he said, followed by a dramatic sigh. "Now, where were we? Heavens, I forget. It doesn't matter. Let's shift our energy to an improvisation exercise. Everybody participates, so please break up in pairs."

Jane was wiping the residual clown white from her face with a Burger King napkin when *he* approached.

"Try using this."

Looking up Jane found herself face-to-face with the handsome man in the turtleneck sweater offering his cloth handkerchief. Mid-forties, well-groomed, he was new to the class. She thought it strange a man carried a handkerchief in this day and age.

"Thank you," she said, reaching for it.

"Let me," the stranger offered. She hesitated, then Jane closed her eyes and let him dab her face. The cloth felt soft. She caught the scent of his cologne, or maybe it was aftershave, and breathed it in.

"I think I got it all."

"Thank you."

"I'm Cooper."

"Jane."

"Jane...?"

"Jane Innes."

"Cooper Sinclaire."

They shook hands. His grasp was firm. *Something about him.*

Cooper nodded towards Jeremy, "I think he likes you."

"I don't think so. He picks on me all the time."

"Need a partner?"

After class Cooper found her, said, "I know a great place where we can get something to eat."

"I don't know...I have to meet a friend," she said. This was her conditioned response, the excuse she'd often used when men hit on her.

"Cancel."

"Maybe some other time." She didn't know anything about him. He was older than any of the men she'd dated before.

"You must be hungry. Just a quick bite. No big deal."

He was so confident, so determined, and she felt uneasy. Jane caught herself twirling her hair. "Maybe next week, after class, we can get a cup of coffee or something."

"Tonight, and I won't take no for an answer."

She felt her nipples alert against her thin blouse. She hoped he hadn't noticed that she wasn't wearing a bra, but was pretty sure he had.

CHAPTER 3

White tablecloths, delicate flowers in tiny porcelain vases—Jane and Cooper shared a quiet corner in a quaint bistro tucked away in West Hollywood.

The waiter poured a sample of red wine. Cooper nosed the glass, tasted it, then approved with a nod. The waiter distributed equally and was off.

"Tell me about you," Cooper said, studying her.

Jane sipped and could tell it was a good bottle, not the under-five dollar twist-cap vintage she drank regularly.

"What do you want to know?"

"Let's start with where you're from."

Self-consciously she began to talk. She told him about growing up in Albuquerque, an only child with a single-parent mom. She told him about the semester at the University of Colorado when she caught the acting bug, about driving her Nissan out to L. A. to try to make it as an actress. She told him about her different odd jobs. He was especially intrigued by the work she'd done for the private investigator. She told him about the recent Rasputin incident.

"I'm banking hours so I can get my own license," she said. "You can't make any money working for PIs. You've got to be your own boss and bill the hours yourself. I figure it's a gig that will allow me the freedom and flexibility to work as an actress."

"Are there times," he asked, "that you impersonate people?"

"Never in person, but I've done it over the phone."

He waited silently until she explained.

"Once I pretended to be a career headhunter to gather information for one of our clients, a woman attorney who practices family law."

"Oh?"

"A deadbeat dad was skipping out on alimony and child support. They tried to garnish wages but he claimed to be unemployed. I got him to admit he was working under the table, and making a pretty good living. The phone call was recorded and he was subpoenaed to appear in court."

"How'd you get him to spill the beans?"

"I pretended I was really interested in his spa and hot tub business. Flirted a little. Built up his ego and earned his trust, I guess."

"How'd you do that?"

"Listened mostly. Let him brag about himself. Encouraged him. He took the bait."

"I bet you're good at it."

"I guess so. I'm an actress."

"Tell me more."

Jane was careful not to give him too many details. The double-wide trailers she and her mother lived in, the crazy boyfriends she endured, and the fact that she never knew her father. The waiter returned and refilled her glass. She talked about how acting was her complete obsession. All else was secondary.

"I can't seem to get a break," she said.

"It will happen. You're talented," Cooper said. "You're a lot better than everyone else in class."

"Thank you for saying that," she said, feeling a dash of confidence enhanced by the warming effect of the wine. "What about you? Tell me what you've done."

"What I've done?"

"As an actor."

"I'm really kind of new to it all," he said. "I thought it might be fun to try because I've always been a ham."

"But Jeremy doesn't accept just anybody. You had to pass his rigorous audition process to get into the class."

Cooper shrugged. "Sure."

"He must have seen something in you," she said.

"Maybe. I don't know. It's fun." He gave her a playful smile. "I live to have fun. How about you?"

She met his eyes for a moment, had an idea what he meant by that. She looked away without answering, smiled to herself. There was spark and sizzle—a thousand words conveyed in one brief, mischievous moment of silence.

The waiter appeared again with a sliced baguette and duck pate. When Jane took a bite she realized this was the first thing she'd eaten all day, other than three peppermint Lifesavers. Probably why the wine had gone straight to her head.

Cooper drove Jane home that night. His sleek Jaguar made it clear he was wealthy. She liked the smell of the leather upholstery.

When they pulled up outside her shabby apartment complex Jane felt the need to make an excuse. "I lost my roommate and I'm sort of in between places right now."

He made her feel at ease, insisted that he walk her to the front gate. When he asked to see her again Jane fumbled through her bag and gave him a business card with her picture on it, an actor's calling card. When Jane first came to Los Angeles, two years ago, she hired a photographer who specialized in creating eight by ten head shots for budding actors. The cards were part of the package.

"Call this number, it texts me," she explained. "I'll call right back."

Cooper raised his eyebrows.

"I don't have a home phone since this place is a temporary arrangement, and I'm in between cell phones right now because the reception is so bad on this block." The truth was Verizon had shut off her landline months ago, the heartless bastards, and there was no "talk time" credit left on her pay-as-you-go cell phone.

After an affectionate peck on the cheek, Cooper bid Jane goodnight and casually drifted off, a perfect gentleman.

Jane crawled into bed happy. She marveled how her day started out so awful but then, in the blink of an eye, turned so wonderful. For one magical evening she'd been able to forget her troubles.

She thought about him, tried to remember his

scent, definitely in the mood. She imagined he was in bed next to her, and then the endless possibilities.

CHAPTER 4

Fancy dinners, jazz clubs—she ran out of nice things to wear and started borrowing clothes from her neighbor Carla.

Carla Gomez was from La Puente, a Hispanic blue-collar suburb east of Los Angeles. She worked as a bank teller and moonlighted as a hostess in a restaurant nearby. Jane didn't have many friends and considered Carla her closest.

Carla's clothes were more revealing than Jane would have chosen for herself, but they fit well and struck the right note for the upscale places Cooper took her.

"A little black dress is always in style," Carla told her. Carla also owned lots of high-heeled shoes. Jane had claim to only one pair of heels, so she was in luck.

In return Carla demanded all the romantic details. Jane felt giddy, like a teenager, talking about boys from school as she curled up on Carla's couch and filled her in.

"You're so lucky," Carla said. "A nice guy with bucks. That's it, girl."

Jane explained she felt Cooper was very patient, careful not to force himself upon her. Testing the waters, his kisses grew heavier and his hands explored, but he was always respectful, always tender.

"He got any cute friends?"

Cooper and Jane agreed it would be best to keep their dating secret from Jeremy and the acting class. Pretending not to be interested in him was difficult. She stole glances from time to time but after class left separately. They often met for a late dinner, just as they had on their first date.

She was falling hard.

One evening they went to a Beverly Hills nightclub, a dark and cozy piano bar. A jazz trio set the mood as the raspy-voiced female singer belted old-school standards, Peggy Lee and Billy Holiday. The patrons were much older, distinguished.

After a few scotches Cooper leaned in and whispered to her, "What do you say we cut out of here and stiff the waitress?"

"Why?" Jane asked, confused.

"For the thrill. This place is packed. She won't see us."

"Leave without paying?"

"Haven't you ever stolen anything? Shoplifted?"

"No."

"Let's give it a shot."

"We can't," Jane said, catching sight of the middle-aged cocktail waitress standing at the bar. "I used to wait tables and enough assholes—"

"—But it'll be exciting."

"I've got money," she reached for her purse.

"No, no, put that away. I was only joking." Cooper pulled a wad from his pocket. Jane could see there was a crisp hundred-dollar bill on top. Why would he want to stiff the waitress? It seemed so weird.

Cooper left a generous tip and they were off.

On the way to his car Cooper suggested they go back to his place for a night-cap. Jane had a pretty good idea where that would lead.

He had mentioned that he lived on the West Side so Jane was not surprised when Cooper drove to Marina Del Rey. But she was surprised when he parked and led her past the luxury waterfront apartments to the docks.

"You never said you lived on a boat," she said.

"Guess it never came up."

What a yacht it was. Jane was floored when she stepped inside. The boat was extravagant with polished wood, plush carpet and a good-sized galley.

"It's awesome," she said.

He went to the refrigerator. "Champagne?"

At the counter he popped the cork. She kicked off her heels, and standing behind him, slid her arms around his waist.

"Guess I'll have to call you Captain now, follow orders" she said, teasing, "and be your wench."

He turned and she devoured him with kisses.

It quickly grew more passionate. On the way to the bed Cooper ripped a few buttons from Jane's borrowed dress. She didn't care, groped his shirt and worked her hands down his hard torso. They undressed each other, both breathing heavily.

It was a nice surprise to discover Cooper's well-defined body. She ran her hands down his core, then wriggled her fingers through his pubic hair finding him rock hard.

They hit the sheets.

His skin was warm and soft. She could feel his muscles surge, entangled, quenching Jane's heated desire.

She wrapped her legs around him and they were in union.

It felt so right.

The next morning, after kisses and lattes made from the boat's cappuccino machine, Cooper drove Jane to her apartment.

"You're incredible," he whispered in her ear as they kissed goodbye. She watched him drive off, smitten.

The next day he made no contact with her. Jane tried his cell. She got his voice mail and left a message. Getting no response, and feeling vulnerable, she left another message.

By the time she left the fourth message Jane was miserable.

"Hey, I haven't heard from you so I hope everything's okay. Call me. Miss you."

She hung up hoping her voice was not too desperate, too obvious. *Desperation is the worst perfume,* she once heard. Why didn't he call back?

Later that evening, and under protest, Carla drove Jane out to Marina Del Rey. The night was foggy, the streets damp.

"This is stupid," Carla said. "He's probably married and never told you. Probably got bratty kids, too."

"Maybe, but I have to talk to him."

They traveled down Lincoln Boulevard in Carla's

Mazda and turned on to Tahiti Drive. Jane tried to remember where his boat was docked. She saw the familiar entrance and told Carla to stop.

"Will you come with me?" Jane asked.

"Hell no. You're crazy. Play hard to get, and let him call you. They always do, eventually."

"Come on, it's dark."

"You're such a wimp."

They got out and walked to the gated entrance. It was locked and there was no way to climb over. Then a gay couple came through, well-dressed guys in their forties obviously going out for the night.

"Hello, ladies," one of them said.

"I lost my key," Carla said.

"Sure you did."

"You don't believe me?"

One of them was Hispanic and he and Carla exchanged a few words in Spanish that Jane did not understand. Her charm prevailed. They shared a laugh and Jane caught the gate before it locked.

Approaching the docks she could see Cooper's yacht. The fog was thick. Cabin lights reflected off the black water. Jane moved cautiously, trying not to make any noise.

They peered into a porthole.

Cooper was inside working on his laptop.

"I see him."

Carla offered a nod.

Jane took a moment to collect herself and was about to board the yacht when she saw someone else—in silhouette.

Another woman.

The woman brought Cooper a cup of tea and

affectionately fondled the back of his neck. Cooper kissed the woman on her hand and went back to his work.

Jane and Carla shared a look.

"See. I told ya."

"Shit!" Tears and a salty tang in her throat, Jane was devastated. She ran back and Carla followed.

CHAPTER 5

Jane had performed grand openings before. They did not pay as well as birthday parties but there was no other work on the horizon, and this was a three day gig. Clown-face painted in a frown to match her mood, Jane filled helium balloons outside the entrance of a new Costco.

As down as she was, Jane found it in herself to pantomime a silly story. A few kids stood stone-faced as Jane mimed that it took great strength to keep the helium balloon grounded. Jane reminded herself that every chance to perform is a gift, whether it was a B-movie, bad dinner theater, or occasional work as a clown. In the midst of this performance Jane's phone buzzed in her pocket. She snuck a peek at the display.

It was Cooper.

Her spent cell phone allowed basic texting but the voice calls were blocked until she could refill the account, so she took a break and then gave Cooper a call from the payphone in the lunchroom. As it rang Jane studied the State of California minimum wage placard near the phone.

"Hello?" Cooper answered

"It's me. What do you want?" she said.

"To see you."

"Where've you been?"

"I'm so sorry. I've been swamped with work. I

really should have called you back."

"What do you want?"

"Let's get together. I miss you."

At that moment a handful of Costco employees entered, gossiping and laughing. Jane could see some were taken aback by a clown in their lunchroom.

"I've got to get off the phone, I'm working," she said.

"We need to talk,"

"I'm busy tonight."

"Look, Jane—"

"I've got to get back to work."

She hung up on him.

Jane stepped out of the lunch room and heard the pay phone ringing behind her. Jane tried her best to wipe her tears without smearing her painted clown face.

By the time she was outside her beeper buzzed, Cooper again. She ignored it and returned to her kiosk.

A small girl pointed and said, "Mommy, look at the sad clown."

An hour later Jane saw Cooper in his Jaguar cruising the Costco parking lot. How had he found her? Someone must have picked up the payphone back in the lunch-room and offered her whereabouts. "She's the clown passing out balloons."

Jane darted inside, abandoning her post, balloons floating to the heavens.

There's no way in hell he's going to see me in this corny costume.

At the lockers she got her clothes, changed in the restroom and left out back through the tire center.

Up the street Jane caught the bus, and on the way home wondered if she would be fired for leaving.

Back in her studio apartment, Jane opened the bottle of Bolla Chianti she was saving, swallowed a gulp and got into a hot shower. She finished a good cry under the spray and felt better. She slipped into her terry-cloth robe, combed her hair and poured more Chianti.

Not the first time her heart had been broken. But this time her feelings for Cooper were so intense, so real. She'd felt alive. Why does it have to hurt so much?

She turned on the television and was mildly caught up by a police pursuit. The news helicopter followed a pick-up truck in a reckless get away. Jane could recognize some of the freeway exits as the guy eluded capture. Someone knocked on her door. She turned down the volume and peeked out of the curtains.

It was Cooper. He caught sight of her. "Jane?"

"What do you want?" Jane asked.

"It's me."

"So?"

"Let me in so we can talk."

"No."

"What's wrong?"

She opened the door a crack, peeked out. "I saw you with her," she said with venom.

She could see his wheels turning.

"On your boat. Is she your wife?"

"My wife?"

"The woman I saw!"

"No, she's not my wife."

"You don't return my calls, and you're seeing someone else. I don't need that shit, all right? And I'm busy right now, so—"

"—Look, I just want to talk. Can I come in?"

"No. My place is a mess."

"Just give me a chance to explain."

"There's nothing to explain."

"Let me in and we can talk about it. I don't know what you saw, but it's not what you think. You need to know something. It's important."

Jane unchained the lock and stepped away from the door.

He let himself in and closed it gently.

She cleared fashion magazines from her couch so he had a place to sit. She debated offering him wine since she was drinking.

"Look," he said, "I'm sorry I didn't call you. And that woman you saw, she's not a girlfriend either."

"I've heard that before. Look, I don't play second fiddle."

"How can I explain it to you—?"

"—You don't have to explain anything." Jane took a healthy sip of her wine.

"She's an actress."

"Oh, Christ," she said, on the edge of tears.

He reached over and took the sleeve of her robe. "Please, bear with me for a moment," he said. "I'm sorry I haven't been honest with you. That woman you saw was an actress from another class. I'm in a few acting classes, not just Jeremy's, but for good reason. I'm searching for the right partner. Can you keep a secret?"

On television the cops fish-tailed the pick-up. The guy was out of the truck, running, vaulting a chain link fence. Cops and dogs closed in.

Cooper continued. "I'm searching for the right partner. If I don't find her I'm going to miss a great opportunity. I'm looking for a collaborator to pull a job."

"What kind of job?"

"An illegal job."

Jane said nothing.

"Listen, I'm not in real estate like I said. I'm looking for a partner to play the part of my wife in order to pull this thing off. It's going to be risky."

"And illegal. Got it."

"A con. A swindle involving diamonds."

"Diamonds?"

"I need a shill."

Jane knew what a shill was from her experience doing magic tricks but she questioned him anyway. "What's a shill?"

"A plant. A person who appears to be an outsider. Someone who seems trustworthy to the mark."

Jane also knew what a "mark" was—a term familiar in the magic trade. She tried to make sense of it all, said to him, "So you're a con man?"

"I prefer to be called a craftsman in the art of deception."

His big yacht, fine clothes, it was now clear. "The boat's not yours, am I right?" she asked.

"Leased. Look I'm sorry I lied to you. Sometimes I just—-It doesn't matter."

She studied him.

"Unfortunately you're only half of what I'm looking for. You're beautiful and you radiate such goodness. But I don't think you've got the nerve, the moxie. I'm not sure if I see it in you. That's why I'm still searching."

She studied her carpet not knowing what to say.

"I messed up." A hint of emotion was weaving into his voice. "I started to fall in love. I didn't mean for that to happen."

"That time you wanted to stiff our waitress," she asked, "was that a test?"

"Yes. You didn't pass, but you were honorable."

On television the cops had the perpetrator handcuffed and face down in an alley. He squirmed but was going nowhere.

"I really shouldn't have told you so much. I just felt I owed it to you. Can you keep my secret?"

"Yes."

"Promise?"

"I promise."

"Thank you." He rose and turned to go.

"How illegal is this thing you're doing?" she asked.

"I've said too much."

"Does this other girl, that actress on your boat, does *she* have the moxie?"

"I'm sorry. Goodbye."

He let himself out.

Jane sank into her couch. *A con man?* She was lost in the notion of it all.

On television the cops escorted the bad guy to their patrol car and the station returned to its regular programming.

On day two of her clown gig she found Clifford "Wizzbo" Nance at her balloon kiosk. She knew Wizzbo, heavy and balding, always in a pathetic costume. For the children he put on a goofy and comical act, but around adults Jane found him caustic and cynical.

"Clifford?" she said approaching.

"What are you doing here?" he said, eyeing the clown wig peeking out of her bag.

"I was about to ask you the same question."

"Haven't you heard?" He leaned in and burped, his breath smelling of beer. "You're fired."

"You're my replacement?"

"They say you freakin' up and split. What's with that?"

Anger flared but she tried not to show it. She turned on her heels and headed back to the bus stop.

"I say something wrong?" Clifford called out.

When Jane returned to her apartment she was shocked to see an eviction notice posted on her door. Eviction? How was that possible? She was only one month behind in rent.

She knocked on the apartment manager's door. Squat Mrs. Kovacs answered. She wore a sweatshirt featuring frolicking garden gnomes.

"What's this?" Jane asked showing her the notice.

"Yes, I know, Jane. There's nothing I can do." Miss Kovacs was from Eastern Europe, her accent thick.

"But I thought we had an agreement. I told you, I can pay half and make it up next month."

"It is not my doing, darling. The new property management company, they insist. They say you are behind in rent so often that you've broken your lease, and want you out for good."

"But I can make it up. If you just give me some time."

"The new property management, I tell them this for you, darling. But they say *no*, they say it is new policy. I'm so sorry, Jane. Are you hungry? I've made chicken dumplings. Come, please, come in and eat."

Jane said nothing more and returned to her apartment. Sitting on her couch, the eviction notice in her hand, she thought about what Cooper had said. He was searching for a partner in crime to do something illegal, he made that clear. But Jane was trained as an actress, and playing a part in his scheme could be the role of a lifetime.

His wife, this shill, it's a part. This is an acting job.

Cooper needed someone to play a convincing character. It would be a flawed character, an accomplice, but flawed characters are the best kind. And deep down Jane knew she could play this role. *I can bring the character to life.*

She picked up the phone to call Cooper but remembered Verizon had shut off her service. In the drawer where she kept her laundry detergent she found enough quarters for a phone call.

She walked to the 7-Eleven.

She waited until sirens cleared in the distance before calling on the payphone. She was planning on leaving a message but was surprised when Cooper answered.

"It's me. Tell me more about this job."

CHAPTER 6

Cooper said he couldn't talk business over the phone. He had sent a car service for her but the Lincoln she had ridden over in was gone now. Jane was punching Cooper's security code into the polished brass keypad of the gated entrance when she sensed the men behind her. They were watching.

Frantic, she punched the four-digit code a second time before the buzzer finally sounded. She entered. The heavy gate clanged shut behind her. She broke into a run until she reached Cooper's boat.

"I think those men are following me."

They walked casually by, one waving to Cooper.

"Hey, Coop," he said.

"Taking her out today?" Cooper called out to them.

"Catalina for the Avalon Blues Festival."

"Nice."

Jane felt foolish for not recognizing them from the night she was here with Carla.

"Louis and Jim," he said. "They've got the thirty-two footer."

She let out a sigh. "I thought they were...I was sure they were following me."

"They're quite harmless...um, a couple, if you know what I mean. Nice guys."

"My active imagination."

"Let's eat."

In the galley down below Cooper made tuna-fish sandwiches on toasted rye. Jane, sitting at the dining table, opened a manila folder. There was a photo of a man in his fifties, stocky with a rugged face. He wore a stylish business suit and scowled to the camera.

"He looks mean," she said.

"Wolff is not known for his kindness or sense of humor."

"His name is Wolff?

"Alexander Wolff, real estate tycoon. Moves fortunes."

"Moves?"

"Like Bobby Fischer, the chess player, that's how Wolff rolls. Aggressive strategy, with speed and a take no prisoners style. Rook takes knight. Sacrifice the pawn. Go in for the kill. As much as I skirt the law now and again, Wolff makes me look like a pure amateur."

"How much *do* you skirt the law?"

"I only go after those who can afford it."

"And Wolff can afford it?"

"In spades. He also brokers in bonds, precious metal, off shore investments, but real estate mostly. He owns high-rises all over the world, many in Hong Kong. Oil wells. And he loves horse racing. Owns a stable of promising thoroughbreds."

"Hong Kong? Is he British?"

"South African and very serious about his privacy." Cooper set the toasted tuna-fish sandwich on the table and took a seat. He poured her lemonade and continued, "He purchased a prized

36

thoroughbred yearling last year in Lexington, Kentucky, and he's coming out here to race it."

Cooper produced a picture of a horse standing in an auction ring and said, "It's got considerable pedigree. His sire won The Dubai World Cup."

Jane sipped her lemonade and asked, "So how does it work, this scam?"

"I propose a diamond deal."

"Diamonds are a girl's best friend."

"Excuse me?"

"Marilyn's life was so sad, when you think about it."

"Who?"

"Marilyn Monroe."

"What's that have to do with anything?"

"It doesn't."

"Pay attention. I'll whet his appetite with real diamonds then swap out for phony, counterfeit stones. Afterward he'll be too embarrassed to go to the cops."

"How's that?"

"To not compromise his image as a world-class deal maker."

Jane took a bite of her sandwich, chunks of pickle mixed into the tuna salad. It reminded her of the way her mother used to make them. "What makes you think he'll go for the scheme?" she asked.

"For a con to work, the mark has to have one distinctive character trait." Cooper paused for dramatic effect. "That, Miss Innes, is greed. Alexander Wolff drips it from his pores, and he's got a monster ego. The horse racing proves he's a gambler. His greed will lead him to our trap. His ego will keep him from squealing afterward."

Cooper was so confident. She felt comfortable sitting next to him, like somehow she belonged there.

"Why me? I mean, there has to be other women...professionals."

"I considered that. But I'm betting he won't suspect you."

"Why not?"

"You have an innocence."

"I'm not all *that* innocent," she said.

Cooper pulled out another file and handed it to her—the image of a beautiful woman on a polo field, high cheek bones and long silky black hair. She was exquisite—could be in one of the fashion magazines back at her apartment.

"That's Alexander's fiancé," Cooper said.

"She's beautiful."

"Alexander Wolff is impossible to get close to. He's evasive and cold, very guarded. The best have tried, salesmen, bankers, nobody can get near. But Veronica is different, more down to earth. That's how we'll get to Wolff." He rested his hand on the top of hers. "That's your job. The entire deal rests on your ability to make her acquaintance, and then become her friend to earn her trust."

Jane studied the picture, trying to imagine what Veronica would be like in real life.

"Veronica is a biblical name," she said. "The woman who cleansed Christ's face at a station of the cross." Jane remembered that from catechism.

"I suppose. We've got to create a random, off-hand encounter. You'll befriend her and set up a dinner. I'll take over from there."

"Why would she want to be my friend?"

"Listen," Cooper leaned in, "that kind of thinking, wipe it out of your mind. You've got to be positive that she'll want to know you."

"Why?"

"I'm going to train you, make you absolutely convincing as a woman from a sophisticated background, having been privileged all your life. I'll tell you what to say and how to say it. She'll *want* to know you."

Jane studied the photographs.

"If you are going to do this," Cooper said, "then I have to make one thing clear."

She met his eyes.

"You've got to do everything I say, without hesitation. Do you understand? No matter what." He sat back waiting for her reply.

"I understand," Jane said. She finished her lemonade. Out of nervousness she chewed the ice. "I need six hundred bucks to fix my car, and another fifteen hundred to catch up on my rent."

"Your rent?"

"And I need three hundred and sixty for the phone company," she said. "And I owe my neighbor Carla about five hundred bucks."

"Don't worry about that."

"Then forget it!" Jane said, angered. "Find yourself another shill."

Cooper burst out laughing. "Hold on. Don't worry. I'll take care of everything. You're not going to need to pay rent because you'll be staying with me. And you won't need a car because we'll drive together. You're going to leave your old life behind."

"But I owe that money, and I want my car."

"Fine, but you can't drive it."

"Why not?"

"It will stick out. Remember, you're someone completely different, a refined young lady, royalty. You're right; you'll need some walking around money." He peeled off a few hundred-dollar bills from his money clip, laying them on the table in the condensation mark of her glass. "If it makes you feel better, I understand your scruples."

"What about my stuff?"

"We'll put your things in storage." Cooper picked up the money and held it out to her, meeting her eyes again. "Take it."

Jane hesitated. Deep inside something told her not to reach for the bills. But something tugged from the other direction. If she accepted his money she would be obligated, his employee. If she didn't she could still walk away.

"Well?" he asked.

Jane took the money.

The new bills were crisp. Jane took her wallet from her purse and placed them inside. "How much are we going to make?" she asked.

"Let's talk about that in the car. We've got some shopping to do."

CHAPTER 7

They drove over Mulholland Pass and dipped into the San Fernando Valley. Smog reigned and long-range visibility was low—a blanket of brown haze seemingly trapped forever.

"How much?" Jane asked.

Cooper rubbed his chin, teasing, as if deep in thought. "Hard to tell because math is not one of my strengths. I figure twenty percent of the take is your end."

"Why not fifty-fifty?"

"Because I cover the expenses, I've done all the leg work and I'm the boss. You're lucky to get twenty. I got five percent on my first job, and was grateful as hell."

Thirty minutes later Jane stood before an assortment of pistols neatly arranged in a glass case.

"Which one do you like?" Cooper asked.

She studied them, some black, others chrome. They stood in the showroom of the VIP Gun Club, an exclusive indoor shooting range housed in a reinforced cinderblock industrial park building in Simi Valley. She could hear occasional muffled shots fired beyond the diamond-plate steel door.

"I've never shot a real gun," she said.

"I don't expect you'll ever have to. But just in case, as insurance, you're going to buy one."

"I could never shoot anyone."

"Like I said, you won't have to."

"Then why do I need one?"

"For protection."

"Protection from what?"

"Think of it as an ace in the hole. Nobody needs to know you have it. It will give you a sense of security, and confidence. You'll always be in control. And if you ever get in a pinch..."

"Do you carry a gun?"

"When I'm working."

"Are you carrying one now?"

"We're not working yet." He glanced down at the case. "I say you give that Colt Auto a whirl," he said, pointing to a .32 chrome pistol with white pearl handles.

Jane considered the weapon. It looked harmless enough.

"It's small enough to fit in a purse," he added.

Moments later, standing in the indoor shooting range, the gun felt snug in her hand. The steel was cold and it was heavier than it looked. He taught her how to insert the clip, hold the gun, aim.

He'd bought ammunition and a paper target of a man's torso, a silhouette of a scowling hoodlum pointing a gun, the bulls-eye highlighted by black oval rings in the middle of the man's chest. Jane thought it sad that the paper target was of a human being, not a round target, like in archery. An automated pulley sent the paper target out to fifty feet.

"Okay. Give it a try."

Jane hesitated.

She had once shot a prop gun loaded with blanks in the movie she acted in, a low budget science fiction film titled *Gemini*. In between takes a professional gun wrangler swapped the pistols loaded with blanks with identical plastic ones for rehearsals and wider shots. But this weapon had real bullets. It scared her.

"Come on," Cooper urged her. "You can do it." He wrapped his arms around her.

She raised the gun, aimed and pulled the trigger.

It was loud, even with her earmuffs on. But after a while Jane got the hang of it. She was surprised by the power of the thing.

When they were out of ammo he led her back to the counter.

They registered the gun in Jane's name. Cooper explained that both the Brady Bill and California law required that the handgun remain at the store for two weeks after the purchase. The FBI would run a background check. Since she didn't have a criminal record she'd be allowed to return and pick up the gun in a "fortnight," the actual word he used. Jane knew that was a term from Shakespeare, heard that expression since working on *Gemini*. The director was nicknamed "Johnny Fortnight" because he had made so many low-budget genre films, most of them shot in just two weeks.

"It's called the cooling off period," the bearded old man behind the counter explained.

Cooper helped her fill out the paperwork then paid for the gun with cash. She had never seen him use cash before, only credit cards. Back in the Jaguar, he said, "Okay, now that we've got that taken care of, let's get you something to wear. Dress you up a bit."

"Dressed to kill?" she asked.

"Precisely."

CHAPTER 8

The silk felt cool against her skin. As the dress caressed Jane's torso when she moved the feeling made her quiver. She felt so sexy, aroused. She could not recall ever having worn anything so beautiful.

Cooper had taken her to an exclusive boutique in Beverly Hills. She was trying on a delicate evening gown in front of the mirror, backless, provocative, yet classy.

"What do you think?" Cooper asked, studying her.

"It's incredible!"

"You'll need heels with that." He turned to the haughty saleswoman, "She's going to need the right kind. And an evening wrap."

"Of course."

Jane knew her type, a middle-aged retail professional wearing Chanel No. 5—hair in a tight bun and skewered with an ivory chopstick.

"Just look at you," Cooper said. "Beautiful."

She looked in the mirror. The last time she felt like this was prom night.

The saleswoman returned with the shoes, then later a sleek designer business suit, skirt cut high. Cooper said he liked the way this "number" accentuated Jane's shapely legs. The saleswoman was quick to produce Italian leather black pumps.

Jane barely recognized herself.

As the saleswoman was busy ringing up the items Jane took him by the hand and led him into the dressing room.

"What are you doing?"

"Ssshh," she said closing the door.

Intoxicated, she unbuttoned his pants then worked her hands below his waist.

"Jane, I don't think..."

To silence him she bit his lip as playful punishment so it was clear she was leading this dance. She worked her mouth around the back of his ear.

She could feel him getting hard.

She stripped her panties off, dropped them at her heels.

"What about...?"

"That bitch can wait," she whispered in his ear.

She pulled his slacks down, and then his briefs. She propped one of her legs up on the bench and he grabbed her behind. His warm hands squeezed tight.

She wriggled until they found each other.

Jane stared at herself in the mirror, said, "Say my name."

"Jane," he whispered.

"Louder"

He complied.

"No. Louder. Say it so the saleslady hears."

Hearing him shout her name at this moment was incredibly exciting. He took charge, increased the pace. She let herself go.

She tried to watch herself in the reflection until

the sensation became so intense and she had to close her eyes. The climax came quick and strong. It was *so good*, powerful—a release that brought tears. She bit his neck, her mouth wet. Cooper maneuvered her into the corner, pressing her bare ass against the glass, holding up one of her legs, driving.

This new position paid off in spades—a jackpot. She came again. He followed soon after. Bar none—this was the best orgasm she'd ever had.

CHAPTER 9

With Cooper's money Jane was able to pay her overdue tuition and Jeremy ceased picking on her. In class Jeremy showed little encouragement toward Cooper but took credit for Jane's newfound confidence.

"This boldness, the strong convictions," Jeremy said, "these fresh choices you've brought to your work, they complement you, my dear. And you wear them well. You are progressing well in my class."

Cooper and Jane shared a glance. Jane knew all this was Cooper's doing. He had reshaped her. He was the one who'd created the new persona.

Later that night on the boat Cooper gave Jane her new name: Kimberly VanCise. "Old money, Dutch-Catholic," he said. "That's you."

"Tell me more about her."

"Refined. Educated. She's graceful, cares for others, yet knows how to have a good time. She's unpretentious."

"What'd she study?"

"Russian literature. Know anything about that?"

"A little about Chekhov's plays."

"That's a start."

"Where'd I go to school?"

"Brown University. Ivy League but not too obvious. You got a Masters, but don't mention that unless it comes up."

"I got a Masters?"

"Your trust fund encouraged a higher education."

These few details sent Jane's imagination whirling. She asked, "What's your name going to be?"

"Charles VanCise."

"Like that. It's got a ring to it."

The next day Cooper and Jane moved her things out of her apartment and into a nearby storage unit. She paid Carla the money she owed, and told her that she was going out of town on an acting job. Close enough to the truth, really. Carla was happy for Jane and wished her luck.

Cooper and Jane no longer spent evenings out. He insisted she study her background, read Tolstoy and Dostoyevsky, and undergo rigorous training. He taught her to walk and talk. He spent hours on her table manners since, as he put it, "so much of the time we will spend with both Wolff and Veronica will be over meals."

Gone was their courtship; this was schooling.

One morning Cooper's cell phone rang. Jane looked on as Cooper nodded and listened intently. He got up and paced while on the phone. It was clearly the tip he'd been waiting for.

"Great. Thank you." Cooper hung up and turned to Jane. "Alexander Wolff is going to be here in three days."

"Veronica, too?

"Yes. We don't have much time."

CHAPTER 10

Alexander Wolff had reservations at the Bel Air. Jane knew the hotel was known for two things: a famous bar where countless Hollywood deals were supposedly negotiated, sometimes on the back of a cocktail napkin, and an exceptional spa that rivaled those found in the luxurious desert retreats of Arizona or Palm Springs. Cooper assumed Veronica would spend time in the spa. This is where Jane would make her introduction. When he insisted they do a preliminary scout of the location, Jane put on her new business suit and tied up her hair.

After driving up a tree-lined road into Bel Air they arrived to face a spiffy brigade of valets, tanned college-aged guys who could easily be fashion models, Jane thought. They opened Jane's car door and handed Cooper a ticket with white-toothed smiles.

What first caught Jane's eye was the hotel's expansive grounds and meticulous landscaping. They passed through the garden lobby and moved to the bar for a drink.

Cooper ordered for her. "The lady will have a cosmopolitan, and bring me a Woodford Manhattan, straight up." When the waitress left he turned to her and said, "As Kimberly, you'll order only cosmopolitans or Absolute Martinis. Don't ever ask for wine."

"But I like wine," she said.

"Not knowing wine reeks bourgeois. It's a dead give-away."

"I know my wine."

"Not the wine that Kimberly drinks. Trust me."

She figured he was right and asked "What's in a cosmopolitan, anyway?" having only read about them in fashion magazines.

"Vodka, cranberry, triple sec. It's what debutantes drink. You'll like it."

"Kimberly would drink it?"

"Since college. And also, forget those Lifesaver candies you eat all the time. Kimberly wouldn't do that."

"Okay," she agreed, knowing deep down she'd miss them.

When the drink came Jane sipped it with apprehensively but was pleasantly surprised. It really did taste good. All it took was this little detail, this sensory hit of flavor enhanced by alcohol and her character kicked in.

She was no longer Jane Innes. She was now Kimberly VanCise. It felt great. She sat up taller—a new persona.

Cooper asked for the menu from the hotel's restaurant and showed Jane not only what to order, but how to order it. He also said she must make a mental note of the first names of the hotel staff without having to rely on their name-tags. It would not only encourage them to remember hers, but imply that she stays at the hotel often.

Kyle Foster, a successful actor in his twenties she recognized from the movies, entered the bar with an entourage of friends, hipsters and all under-dressed for the place. They settled into a booth in the rear.

Cooper caught Jane checking them out. "You know him?"

"That's Kyle Foster."

"Who?"

"He's a movie star. He used to date Jessica Sanchez."

Cooper craned his neck. "I don't see many movies."

Jane realized Cooper was from another generation. How could he not know Kyle Foster? Veronica, their mark, was a good twenty years younger than Alexander Wolff judging from the photos Cooper had shown her. She glanced around the bar. With the exception of Kyle and his jean-clad friends, Jane could see most of the men were with women much younger. Were these men's second or third wives? Mistresses? That's the difference between the "haves" and the "have-nots," she thought.

It was the first time she'd ever thought of Cooper as being old.

"Finish up, beautiful," he said, "let's take a stroll." She liked that he called her beautiful.

They walked by one of the pools and he pointed out the exclusive bungalows adjacent to the main hotel.

"That's where Wolff stays," Cooper explained. "We can keep an eye on his room from the pool."

On their way out Cooper stopped at the front desk and confirmed details of Wolff's reservation. Outside he tipped the valet a twenty dollar bill and minutes later they were in the Jaguar.

Gliding down the hill he asked, "So, what was her name?"

"Who?"

"Our waitress at the bar."

"This a test?"

"Were you paying attention?"

"Maureen. Irish name."

"You're going to do fine."

Jane put her hand on the inside of his leg, something Kimberly would do, as they rolled down the hill and out of Bel Air.

The next week Cooper spent a lot of time on his computer, and Jane practiced her new persona day and night. She walked in character, ate in character, spoke and laughed in character. Little mannerisms and details blossomed. Kimberly was starting to function on her own, surprising Jane sometimes.

The character was taking on life.

A FedEx package arrived, and Cooper received new credit cards, all inscribed with an alias. Jane asked him how he did it but Cooper merely said, "You'll learn in time."

Finally the day came. They packed their things and moved into the hotel.

The room was the standard deluxe suite. But Jane had never stayed in a place like this before. The carpet was fine-weave wool, the bathroom marble, the fixtures gold-plated. As she was hanging her new clothes in the closet, her cell phone buzzed. She did not recognize the number so decided to check her voice mail. She picked up the hotel phone and was about to dial when Cooper stopped her.

"What are you doing?"

"Checking my messages."

"Not from this phone. The hotel keeps a record of every call."

"Oh, right. Sorry." Jane felt so dumb.

"Use my cell," he said giving her his phone. "We'll never use that phone, unless it's room-to-room, or to the desk. Understand?"

"Yes."

"Good."

Jane dialed and listened. It was a message from her mother.

"*Hi, Jane, we're here in Los Angeles. Call me. I want to see you, honey.*"

Deflated, Jane sank into the bed.

"My mom, she's in town."

"Where?"

"In Pomona. At the Winter Nationals."

"What's that?"

"A drag race." Jane was so embarrassed. "Her boyfriend is on the Winston Cup Racing Team. They travel the circuit this time of year."

"Listen Jane, I—"

"Don't worry; I'm not going to call her back." She stood and went back to hanging up her clothes, feeling him watch her.

"I think you should," he said.

"Should what?"

"Call her back. If not, she'll worry. If she thinks you're missing, she may call the cops and that wouldn't be good."

"She'll insist on seeing me. I can't get out of it."

"I'm sure we can carve out time." Cooper checked his watch. "Wolff's flight has arrived. They should be here any time now. Come on."

Cooper led Jane into the bar and sat a table with a view of the front desk. Jane ordered a cosmopolitan. Cooper reached into his jacket and pulled out two rings.

"Put these on," he said.

Jane gasped. One was a wedding band, the other a diamond engagement ring.

"We're supposed to be married."

"Oh, right," she said. Tears welled up but she had to remind herself this was not real. Cooper was not proposing to her. This was all part of the role, and these beautiful rings were mere props.

As time passed her nerves got the best of her.

"You all right?" Cooper asked,

"Butterflies," she said.

"Butterflies?"

"In the stomach. Dress rehearsal."

"Oh." Cooper laughed. "Don't worry, we won't approach them tonight. We're just taking a look."

As if on cue Jane watched the bellman cross the lobby and step outside. Car doors slammed. Voices echoed. After a moment Veronica and Alexander Wolff made their entrance.

"There they are," Cooper whispered.

Wolff entered the lobby first. Jane could tell he was a man who'd spent most of his life in charge of things. The woman with him was hidden behind a tall, dark younger man with a shaved head carrying luggage—a bodyguard, Jane guessed.

Then she got a good view of the woman. Jane's first thought was that Veronica was more beautiful in person. She was taller than she appeared in the photograph. As she walked she led with her hips in a fluid motion. Like a swan, or a doe—sensual. It reminded Jane of something she once had learned in acting class; that when breaking down a character the actor should make the choice to lead with either hips, head, or heart. Veronica led with her hips.

As quickly as they'd come, they were gone. The bell staff followed with carts of luggage.

Jane released a deep sigh.

Cooper turned to her. "What do you think?" he said.

"Bring it on," Jane said before downing the last of her drink.

CHAPTER 11

Jane was up early. The light was soft in their hotel room, the sheer drapes casting a faint glow. She could hear birds chirp outside and an occasional door slam down the hall. Jane settled into the plush sofa and was reading the complimentary *New York Times* when Cooper stirred under the duvet cover and sat up.

"You sleep alright?" she asked.

"Why?"

"You were tossing and turning all night."

Without answering he got up, scratching himself and staggering to the bathroom. "Order room service," he said before closing the door.

She could hear the shower turn on as she searched for the menu. Appalled at the exorbitant prices, Jane kept it simple. She ordered the continental breakfast for two which included a pot of coffee. Coffee was what she needed most.

Jane turned on the television. In silence, she and Cooper watched the morning news while eating breakfast.

"You might think about getting ready," he said.

Countdown to curtain, she thought.

Jane fell back on her training to transform into character as she changed into her costume. She did this now, concentrating on how Kimberly would dress herself. Cooper had ordered cotton drawstring pants and a Brown University sweatshirt. Jane had washed the sweatshirt a few times to make it feel worn-in. By the time she eased into her sandals, she was ready.

"Good luck," Cooper said.

"You're not supposed to say that!"

"Why not?"

"You're supposed to say 'break a leg.' You should know that."

"Oh. What else am I not supposed to say?"

"A lot of things."

"Like?"

"The name of the Scottish Play in a theatre."

"What's that?"

"Shakespeare's *Macbeth*."

"Why not?"

"It's bad luck."

"Who says?"

"Forget it." She kissed him, a quick peck on the cheek—not her style, but the way she envisioned Kimberly would kiss her husband Charles goodbye.

Walking through the hotel she was a little nervous, which she knew was good—like an athlete before an event. She was ready for the challenge.

Jane strolled outside, crossed a bridge over a delicate koi pond, and entered the Asian-themed spa. A pleasant young woman with a perfect complexion greeted her at the reception desk, jotting down her name and room number. Jane declined the offer for a deep tissue massage and scanned the place. There were a few women lounging in the waiting area reading or watching television, but no Veronica. An attendant gave her a thick robe and directed her to the changing room.

At a full-length mahogany locker, Jane undressed and slipped into the robe before checking out the sauna, Jacuzzi and whirlpool. In an exercise room a yoga instructor modified the positions of her few students.

Still no Veronica.

Jane kicked off her sandals, disrobed and slipped into the Jacuzzi. The water was hot and took getting used to. She submerged her body in stages until she was neck deep and had a good view of the place. Jane closed her eyes. This is how it feels to be Kimberly.

Moments later Jane was startled to see Veronica moving toward the Jacuzzi wrapped in a terry cloth robe. She watched out of the corner of her eye as Veronica disrobed near Jane. She could see Veronica was in excellent shape, her back muscles shapely, and her legs long and firm.

Jane closed her eyes again, and opened them when she felt Veronica slip in the water on the opposite side of the Jacuzzi.

"Good morning," Jane said.

"Hi," Veronica said, adjusting her hair into a ponytail.

Jane casually glanced away, searching for a way to open the conversation, something off-hand.

But then Veronica spoke first. "I love these places."

"This one's really nice," Jane said.

"Have you ever been to Canyon Ranch?" Veronica asked.

"That's in Arizona, right?"

"Just outside Tuscon."

"I haven't, but friends say it's great."

"I highly recommend it."

Jane said nothing and considered her next move. Cooper taught her it was best not to lead the conversation, but steer it. Small talk was one thing, but she knew she would have to get to a more intimate place, a commonality between them.

"My husband's here on business.... what brings you to Los Angeles?" Jane asked.

"Same. My fiancé has meetings all week."

"Where are you from?" Jane asked.

"Cape Town, but I grew up in New York."

"Oh. Did you live in the city?"

"Raised upstate, but I met Alexander in Manhattan, when I used to live there."

She offered me his name. That was a good sign.

"Charles and I met in the city as well. At an auction at Christie's." Jane felt good that Cooper's alias rolled off her tongue so easily. "He outbid me for a signed first-edition of Jane Austen's *Pride and Prejudice* and I was furious. Then he asked me to lunch, the rascal. Do you make it to New York often?"

"Not as often as I'd like."

Jane made idle conversation about a number of things, all rehearsed—her supposed ski chalet in Sun Valley, her supposed education and travels. When Veronica broached the subject of movies Jane was glad. This was something she could talk freely about without having to fake it. They chatted about various stars and Hollywood gossip.

As they became acquainted, Jane found Veronica

to be surprisingly laid back, and she seemed like a lot of fun. They moved to the sauna and then to the whirlpool. Finally the two retreated to separate showers. Jane finished quickly, and was dressed when Veronica emerged from the frosted glass stalls and moved to the sink.

When Veronica was brushing her jet-black hair Jane figured she'd take a stab at it. "Since we're both staying here maybe we should arrange a dinner some evening. My husband would love to commiserate with a fellow New Yorker," Jane said.

Veronica looked over in the reflection of the mirror. "I'll ask if Alexander's got the time," she said.

"We're in suite three twenty," Jane said and turned to go, "It was really nice meeting you."

"Likewise," Veronica said.

Jane walked briskly back to her room, through the garden and past the pool. She felt good about how it went—the groundwork. Cooper was in the room waiting for her, watching television. He muted the volume as she sat down and recounted every detail.

He listened silently, nodding. Something was definitely wrong. He seemed angry.

"Everything all right?" she asked.

"When were you going to tell me about this?" he asked, motioning to the television. Jane turned and was astonished to see *Gemini*, the B-movie she performed in years ago. Amid explosions and gunfights rebel cyborgs battled mutant troopers. The movie's costumes, special effects and props came off laughably low-budget. On screen Jane was bent over a dying cyborg soldier prying the weapon from his hands. She wore leather pants the tight black-vinyl corset accentuated her breasts.

"I can't believe it," she said, sinking into the chair.

"Is that really you?"

"Oh shit."

"Why didn't you tell me? What if Alexander or Veronica sees this?"

"What are the chances they'll ever—?"

"It's a porno on the hotel pay-per-view!" he said, furious.

Jane was shocked to see another scene spliced in, a futuristic orgy of some kind. A space ship interior was crowded with satin circular beds. These actors were different from the original cast and she did not recognize any of them. It was clear this scene was shot later, or more likely cut in from another picture. An X-rated picture.

"That wasn't part of our movie!"

Jane explained that she'd performed in the low-budget movie years ago but the film had never seen the light of day. She assumed it had been shelved forever. "This other stuff, this porn stuff, that wasn't in the script."

They watched as a big-haired vixen in ridiculous shoulder-pads performed fellatio, servicing a well-endowed space commander.

Jane felt like crying.

"I checked," Cooper said. "There are only three skin flicks on the hotel pay-per-view. This is one of them. If they're into this sort of thing the chances they will see this are good, depending on their preference."

To think *this* movie was on her resume, stapled to the back of her headshot sitting in casting offices all over town. She wished she could call her agent and scream, but she did not have an agent. She felt so betrayed, dirty.

The movie returned to Jane and her leading man, Curtis, retreating through smoky, pipe-filled tunnels. This footage was part of the original script. It all came back to her, a wash of memories.

"We shot that scene at the water treatment plant," she said.

"The what?" he said searching the mini bar.

"The sewer."

"Why doesn't that surprise me?"

CHAPTER 12

The next morning Jane was back in the spa. There was no sign of Veronica. She sat in the lounge area because this gave her a good view of the spa's entrance. She read magazines and sipped green tea. The staff tried again to sell her on their assortment of options: aroma therapy, pedicures and exotic mud baths, but she politely refused.

Finally Veronica appeared, and Jane hid behind a *Vanity Fair* magazine. When it was clear she had moved into the dressing room, Jane gave it a few minutes before getting up. She found Veronica undressing.

"What a nice surprise," Jane said.

Veronica yawned. "Oh, excuse me. I couldn't fall asleep so I watched TV all night," she said.

"Must be jet lag," Jane said hoping Veronica had not explored the pay-per-view choices. They made a plan, decided on a light workout in the gym, a sauna and then the Jacuzzi. It wasn't until they were neck deep in wet beauty-clay, and there was a lull in the conversation, that Jane found the opportunity.

"The four of us *should* have dinner."

"I'll check with Alexander. Tonight is probably best. He's got a hectic schedule the rest of the week."

"Charles will be back early, and the restaurant here is quite good."

"Say eight?"

"Perfect."

She had pulled it off. Cooper would be happy.

A wave of accomplishment came over her, goose-bumps of excitement under the cake of therapeutic mud.

CHAPTER 13

"Damn it," Jane said when she noticed a run in her stockings.

"Slow down." Cooper went to the drawer and handed her a new pair. "You're going to be fine. Keep Veronica amused while Wolff and I talk business. At some point I'll cue you to prompt me. When I nudge you under the table, find a graceful way to urge me to talk about my diamond deal, just like we talked about. I'll play reluctant, but push it. Insist I tell the story. Got that?"

"Yeah," she said. Between the details of her privileged background, what she and Veronica had previously talked about, and now this extra stuff; there was so much to remember.

Jane took her time with the new pair of stockings. She clipped them carefully to the garter on her thigh. They felt so different than nylon. These retro silk-stockings did not cling the same but as nylon, but Jane realized "Kimberly" would wear classic stockings like these. *The costume completes the character.*

Cooper zipped the back of her dress and kissed her bare shoulder. "You're beautiful."

"You keep saying that."

"Because you are."

They walked through the hotel grounds, her heels a challenge on the uneven concrete. It was chilly and the clouds at dusk were a splash of bronze superimposed against a deep cobalt sky.

Jane and Cooper arrived at the restaurant a little early. He tipped the maître d' and requested a private table. He also made it clear that the bill was to come to him.

"Yes, sir, of course," the maître d' said and led Cooper and Jane to the table set inside a bay window overlooking the tropical garden. There was live music in the bar. She recognized the Billy Holiday jazz standard. "*All of me, why not take all of me, can't you see, I'm no good without you.*"

The maître d' led Veronica and Wolff to the table. Wolff's bodyguard brought up the rear. Jane had not seen this intensely handsome man since the evening they checked into the hotel. He hung back as Wolff and Veronica approached.

Jane made the introductions. The men shook hands and exchanged pleasantries. Cooper edged up behind Jane and tended to her chair. He had never done that before. She could see this was Cooper's time to shine.

The waiter took their drink orders and Jane saw the bodyguard drift off. He found a seat at the bar.

"Veronica tells me you two met in the spa," Wolff started in.

"It's heavenly." She hoped that wasn't a stupid thing to say.

That hung there until Veronica broke the ice. "Kimberly and I have so much in common, like we've known each other forever."

Cooper and Wolff began to chat about the stock market. Veronica talked about the shopping she had done that day, what she had seen, and how the selection here in Los Angeles was so different than New York. Jane listened and nodded politely, but her ear was craned toward the men.

Cocktails arrived and the men made small talk about an assortment of things most of which Jane did not understand. Cooper spoke of his supposed background in the shipping industry, explaining that Los Angeles is the busiest port in the West. Jane could see this was his subtle prompt to get Wolff talking about what he did. Wolff admitted he was in commercial real estate investments, and Cooper said that technically he was too.

"The difference is," Cooper said, "my buildings float."

This made Wolff laugh. He sipped his single malt.

Jane could see that Cooper had made some headway. She spoke all the lies that Cooper had taught her, about their travels and the people they'd met. Cooper poured on the charm. He told crazy, fun stories and had the entire table laughing.

Jane caught Wolff's eye on a few occasions. She offered a polite smile and glanced away, fully aware that his gaze lingered.

She waited for Cooper's nudge, the signal to bring up the diamond deal.

Wine, entrees, dessert, finally coffee and cognac; still Cooper had not given her the cue. Maybe he would find another way to bring it up. Then, the dinner almost wrapped-up, the waiter brought Cooper the check. He intercepted the bill perfectly as Jane made conversation with Wolff.

Finally he nudged her.

She waited for a lull then leaned into him. "Darling," she said, "you've got to tell them about your friend Roger, the diamond thing."

"No, they won't be interested in—"

"Diamonds?" Veronica asked.

"It's nothing," Cooper said.

"It's fascinating," Jane said. "Come on."

Cooper played reluctant. Jane urged and he finally gave in. He told a story about a close friend, an old college buddy of from Princeton who moved to Brazil ten years ago and bought a diamond mine. "It turned out to be extremely profitable," he said. "He's built a significant market share but the political climate has changed. The Brazilian government is insisting that Roger pay enormous taxes, even demanding back taxes. In an effort to raise cash, and pay off the corrupt government officials, he plans to liquidate much of his inventory and get out of the business. Because the diamond market is controlled by a few major players, a sudden glut may adversely drive worldwide prices down. As a precaution, DeBeers has made an offer to buy everything from him, lock, stock and barrel, also agreeing to pay his tax bill. But they're only offering twenty cents on the dollar, and Roger is furious. He's convinced DeBeers has bribed officials in the government to chase him off. But at this point he has no choice."

Jane felt the need to improvise so added, "And he's just such a nice guy, really great. So smart and down to earth."

Cooper nodded. "It's a shame," he said. "He has

74

to sell everything and leave the country immediately. So, to Roger's friends and family, whoever can come up with the cash, he's unloading the very best diamonds before they audit his inventory." In a dramatic pause, Cooper sipped his cognac.

Jane noticed that Wolff had leaned forward—interest piqued.

Cooper continued, "He's set aside the very best, flawless or nearly perfect stones. That being the case," Cooper reached across the table and took Jane's hand, "in a few days, it seems, we'll take possession of over two thousand diamonds."

Jane added, "I still don't know what we are going to do with them all."

"Stones of that quality," Cooper said, "A trip to Antwerp and they'll be sold within hours."

"Remember, I've been promised a diamond necklace out of this deal," Jane said to Cooper, another improvisation.

"Did I say that?"

She punched him in the arm. "What selective memory you have," Jane said, and then turned to Veronica, "But I'll settle for a tennis bracelet."

Laughs around the table.

"All of these stones are between one and two karats—engagement ring size, the backbone of the diamond trade," Cooper added. "Engagement rings demand the highest price."

"Well, I guess there's no price on love," Wolff said.

Cooper raised his cognac and proposed a toast. "Well said. Let's drink to love."

"To love," Veronica echoed, raising hers.

They toasted and sipped.

Jane felt Wolff's leg brush up against hers— clearly intentional. She pulled her leg away, pretended not to notice.

CHAPTER 14

As they said goodnight Veronica suggested Cooper and Jane join them at the racetrack Saturday afternoon. Wolff's horse, a two-year-old filly named Turquoise, was scheduled run in her debut race at Santa Anita.

Wolff explained that Turquoise had posted solid workouts. "Bullet works," Wolff called them, "but she's yet to race."

Plans were set; a day at the races.

Cooper and Jane walked back to their room. He put his arms around her and kissed her forehead, complimenting Jane on the job she did.

She decided not to tell him about Wolff's leg brushing hers under the table, instead asked, "Is there any truth in that diamond story?"

"In Thursday's, or maybe Friday's *Wall Street Journal* there's going to be an article about the Brazilian government taxing and regulating diamond mines owned by foreigners," he said. "I've got an associate who's been holding the story until I cue him to submit it. If it runs, and our scheme works, I pay him out of our cut."

"How much?" she asked.

"He'll see a nice bonus. Trust me, it's not the first time a gatekeeper of financial information is slipped a kickback."

"Those flawless diamonds you talked about,

where are we going to get them?"

"No diamond is without some kind of flaw. Even the finest stones have slight imperfections of some kind. It's just a matter of what can be perceived. A few of the diamonds will be real, the rest cubic zirconia."

She peeled off her dress, threw on the hotel's terry cloth robe, and plopped down on the duvet cover. "I'm exhausted."

"Hang that up," he said, pointing to her dress lying on the carpet. "That's professional equipment. Treat it right, damn it."

"Sorry." She got up and hung her dress in the closet. She gathered the silk stockings as well, folding them neatly.

"I feel like a nightcap," Cooper said while taking off his tie. He opened the mini bar and poured himself a scotch without offering her anything.

"Should I go to the spa again tomorrow?" she asked

"No, we don't want to wear out our welcome. Use the day to visit your mother. Take my car," Cooper said.

Jane was relieved. She needed a break.

He sipped his scotch in silence. His mind working, she could see he was in his element.

CHAPTER 15

The next morning Jane was behind the wheel of the Jaguar. The sensation of the luxury automobile gliding with precision felt so different than her Nissan. She cleared downtown and was somewhere near West Covina when a stone smacked the windshield with a loud pop.

"Shit," Jane screamed and changed lanes.

The stone left a dime-sized fracture in the glass. Gunning it, she passed the semi and glanced at the starburst shape—a thin crack on the windshield. Cooper trusted her and now she'd ruined his perfect car.

She was still lamenting the blemish by the time she reached Pomona Raceway.

Following the instructions her mother had given her, Jane maneuvered the Jaguar past the grandstands to a cluster of trailers. She slowed to see men hovering, tinkering with dragsters, some of them checking her out. She drifted through the camp until he found the trailer with "Danny Dobson Racing" painted on the side. Jane got out and her mother came running.

"My baby! My baby Jane!" she squealed, embracing her daughter. "Why look at you!" she said with tears of joy in her eyes. She turned to the trailer. "Danny, come meet my precious daughter."

Danny Dobson, a lean and tanned man in his

late-fifties, emerged from the Winnebago.

"Danny, my daughter Jane."

Danny sized up the Jaguar before he approached. He offered his hand. "It's nice to meet you," he said with a soft-spoken drawl, a tinge of West Texas, Jane guessed.

"It's really nice to meet you, too," Jane said.

They made small talk, and Danny's casual manner put her at ease. She felt good that her mom was involved with a genuinely nice guy. There had been so many bad ones.

After introductions and pleasantries, Nancy and Danny opened the trailer and showed Jane the dragster. Danny explained they were here to attend the NHRA Pomona Winter Nationals. "A lucky qualifying round," he said, "could pencil-out to thousands in purse money and a guarantee sanction for next season." Danny checked his watch and excused himself, apologizing for having to attend a meeting. He grabbed a pack of cigarettes and walked toward the grandstands.

Jane and her mother took a stroll.

"He's good to me," Nancy said, "and we have fun, traveling the circuit, it's an adventure."

"I'm happy for you, Mom."

"Enough about me, tell me about you. You a movie star yet?"

"No."

"That car and your nice clothes. Must be doing well."

"I'm doing a little bit of work here and there."

"Do you have a boyfriend?"

"Yeah. It's his car, not mine."

"Is he good to you?"

"Yeah, he is."

"Then we'll all have to get together. We're here until Monday. You two have to come out Saturday and see Danny race. We'll get you pit passes."

"I can't, Mom, sorry. I'm working, and he's out of town."

"Oh," she said, clearly disappointed. "What's your boyfriend's name?"

"Cooper. I'm sorry we can't make it."

"Nonsense. You can find the time. I want Danny to get to know you."

"I can't," Jane said, getting agitated. Her mom had a way of getting on Jane's nerves. "I'm sorry. Matter of fact, I'll be going out of town for a long time, out of the country."

"Where are you going?"

"A lot of places."

"Sounds exciting."

"Yeah."

There was an awkward silence.

"You and your acting bug," Nancy said. "Just as long as you're happy. That's what's important. Are you happy?"

"I am, Mom."

"I'm glad."

They walked in silence for a while. Nancy pulled out a cigarette and offered one but Jane refused.

Nancy lit hers and said, "Let's sit down for a sec." They took a seat on the bleachers as engines revved in the distance. Nancy took a drag of her smoke. "I know I didn't give you the greatest childhood, moving around as we did. Never had much. I'm sorry."

"Mom, you did great."

"I have my regrets."

"You raised me good," Jane said, realizing she'd used terrible grammar. Her character Kimberly would never speak that way.

"Your father," Nancy said, "I've always told you he was a man who came and went." Nancy paused. "That's true, but only part of the story. Now you're old enough you should know everything."

"Everything what?" Jane asked, wondering where this was leading.

"Before you were born your father went to jail. And that's where he died. He got killed inside. Knifed in a fight. I'm sorry for not telling you sooner."

Jane swallowed hard then said, "For what?"

"I'm not sure what for. Prison is a horrible place."

"No, I mean, what was he in for?"

"He wrote a few bad checks. We were young and dumb. Reckon we partied way too much. I'm sorry I never told you, but I wanted you to know. Just so you can be assured that he won't be coming around. So you can put it to rest."

Jane looked into her mother's eyes, thought about the struggles the two of them endured together, the different men her mother had dated, young Jane in tow. She recalled the fights, the failures and the midnight evictions.

At that moment it became clear, why the desire

to be an actress had been so strong. Acting had always been an escape from her dismal life—a better place to go. And her mother encouraged her every step of the way. The dream was both of theirs.

Jane leaned in and hugged her mom. "You did great, Ma, and I love you."

"Love you too, baby."

Jane sat back and wiped tears. "I have to go."

"So soon?"

"Work. I'm sorry."

"Stay. We'll have dinner. Work can't be that important."

"It is. I'm sorry."

Nancy glanced out over the pavement. The wind blew her hair back and Jane noticed wrinkles in her mom's face she had never seen before.

"Keep in touch," Nancy said, forlorn. "Call, email, or text, whatever." Nancy reached in her jeans and came up with Danny's business card.

Jane took it. "If I can."

"If you can? What's that mean? If you can?" Jane could see Nancy was getting angry.

"Like I said, I'll be out of the country for a while. But don't worry, I'll write, I promise."

Nancy eased, smiled, "I know you will."

They got up and walked back to the Jaguar, hugged a tearful farewell. The last thing Jane heard was her mother say, "Good-bye, my baby Jane. Make me proud."

Driving back Jane could see the chip in the windshield had grown. Like a cancer, she had a feeling this gruesome crack would spread more and more.

She thought about what Cooper had said, how each and every diamond has some kind of flaw, some more than others. Now the Jaguar was imperfect and she knew it was her fault.

She tried to imagine her father. Like a character in a play, or in fiction, she realized he was ultimately flawed—a tragic hero. It all made sense, why she was drawn to Cooper's deceitful plan in the first place. Her inherent flaws, her imperfections were like the crack in the windshield. She'd been born with them—stigma imprinted in her DNA. Immorality was passed down by a man she would never know.

Driving west on Interstate 10 Jane became more and more obsessed with the crack in the windshield. It lengthened more and took shape of a skeleton hand—wretched and cruel.

CHAPTER 16

The diamond necklace was magnificent.

"Where'd you get it?" Jane asked.

Cooper stood behind her at the mirror, clipping the sparkling pendant around her neck. "You claimed were getting a diamond necklace out of the deal, right?" he reminded her. "Well..."

"Yeah, but that was just an ad lib."

"I thought we'd do a little show-and-tell. Don't get too excited. It's cubic zirconia."

She tried to hide her disappointment.

"Let me do the talking," he said. "This time silence is golden, remember."

Jane examined the necklace as they continued to dress, not nearly as enamored now. *Costume jewelry—story of my life.*

She cut the price tags off a new backless dress while Cooper slipped into a freshly laundered shirt. He adorned cuff links and a red tie before reaching for his suit jacket. Moments later they were seated into the Jaguar outside the hotel. Cooper showed no emotion and said nothing when she explained how the window became chipped.

"Shit happens," was all he said.

The plan was to meet Wolff and Veronica at Heidi's, a restaurant in Beverly Hills. Traffic was light. They cruised up Sunset Boulevard into Beverly Hills. She tried her best to forget that hours ago she'd been visiting her mother at a greasy drag strip in the Inland Empire. She tried to imagine what carefree Kimberly would have done with her day, shopping like Veronica, or browsing art galleries.

They arrived at a club just off Rodeo Drive, its entrance hidden from the street. The place was nondescript with a simple brass plaque and a few valets standing at attention.

Inside black marble dominated the modern decor. The space suggested sex and power, track-lighting illuminating delicate orchids, abstract and erotic art hanging on walls of lacquer-black tile. Although Cooper and Jane had arrived early, Wolff and Veronica were already in the bar. The lustrous clientele was predominantly fashion-clad men, and Jane figured most of them were probably gay. She noticed a small dance floor with musical instruments awaiting the band on a stage.

Wolff took Jane's hand and kissed it lightly. "Good evening to you," he said. It seemed so formal and old-fashioned. The Asian hostess led them to their table. Jane spotted Wolff's bodyguard taking a seat at the bar.

Fine wine was carefully poured. Flaming, wondrous gourmet dishes were prepared at their table. The evening felt magical. Cooper made everyone laugh, spinning outrageous stories and Jane marveled at his warmth and ease. After the main course Veronica suggested the women excuse themselves and led Jane to the powder room.

Veronica was touching up her lipstick in the mirror when she complimented Jane on her necklace. "That's an impressive piece you're wearing."

"That Brazilian diamond business my husband is so wrapped up in."

"It's radiant," Veronica said.

"Thank you."

As the women emerged from the restroom the Latin jazz band was starting their set, an upbeat dance groove.

That's when she saw him. Jeremy Sands, her acting coach, was at the bar, out cruising, no doubt.

At that instant Jeremy Sands spotted Jane. He raised his hand in a wave.

Jane turned away and quickened her step.

Veronica noticed this. "Everything all right?" she asked.

Jane knew her knee-jerk reaction was too obvious.

"What is it?" Veronica asked.

"That man," she blurted, nodding to Wolff's bodyguard, also at the bar. "I noticed him at our hotel. I think he's following us."

Veronica turned to the bar and laughed. "That's Buddy. He works for us. He's Alexander's security consultant."

"Security consultant?"

"Bodyguard."

"Oh," Jane said, acting surprised.

"There have been threats," Veronica said, "I told Alexander it's crazy but he's a very cautious man sometimes. He claims it's for my safety too, but I think he's overreacting."

"I'm really not paranoid. It's just..." She could see Jeremy eyeing her.

"Since his name is Buddy, I call him our *buddyguard*," Veronica said, "but he doesn't like that."

Jeremy Sands was still staring.

Jane took her seat and nudged Cooper under the table. Mid-speech and without missing a beat, Cooper picked up on it and glanced to the bar. When he turned back it was obvious that he'd seen Jeremy.

Jeremy got up from his barstool, grabbed his vodka soda and walked to them.

Veronica, meanwhile, was explaining to Jane the differences between her yoga instructors. Jane feigned interest, but her eyes were on Jeremy. Buddy was also on his feet and right behind Jeremy, stride for stride. Both men approached the table at the same time.

"Jane." Jeremy said.

Jane pretended not to notice him. Cooper stood.

"Jeremy, what a surprise," he said. "Excuse us a moment, will you? An old friend," Cooper put his arm around him and led Jeremy away. Buddy stayed where he was, watching them go.

After a few seconds Buddy peeled off, apparently convinced Jeremy was not a threat.

"I love this song," Jane said, then to Wolff. "Would you care to dance?"

Veronica encouraged him with a nudge, "Sure he does. Go."

Wolff seemed surprised. He stood, took her by the arm, and guided Jane to the dance floor. As they blended into the crowd Jane searched for Cooper.

Hips swaying to the Latin rhythm, she could smell his cologne and feel his eyes on her. She wondered where Cooper had gone.

The song came to an end. Cooper was there when they returned to the booth.

"You missed the fun," Jane said.

"Apparently."

"Who was that man?" Jane asked out loud, for the benefit of the others, but then realized it was a mistake because Jeremy had called her by name.

"An old friend. Crazy bastard."

As a round of drinks arrived Jane noticed blood on Cooper's cuff.

"Now it's our turn to dance," Veronica said to Cooper before Jane could clue him in.

"Is that so?"

"Yes, that's so."

They moved to the dance floor leaving Jane and Wolff alone.

"That's a wonderful necklace," Wolff said to her. "Beautiful."

"Thank you," she said. *Less is more,* Jane thought. *Don't say anything.*

She turned and watched the dance floor, fully aware Wolff's eyes were upon her.

CHAPTER 17

In the hotel bar over a nightcap Cooper convinced Wolff to take a look at the stones. It appeared Cooper's charm had taken affect and Wolff was interested in the diamond deal.

"But if we're going to see the stones," he said, "it will have to be in the morning since on Saturdays the bank closes at noon."

"The earlier the better," Wolff said. "Remember, we've got the races tomorrow." He turned to Jane. "I expect you to bring me luck."

"Turquoise," Jane said, remembering the name of his thoroughbred racehorse.

"What time does the race go off?" Cooper asked, as if not interested but entertaining the thought. Jane sensed he was playing hard to get.

"Three or so, but you'll want to get there early. We'll be in the Turf Club."

"Why don't we carpool?" Jane suggested.

"Because we have to be at the stables at eleven," Veronica said, clearly not as enthused.

At this point Wolff waved Buddy over. He introduced him to Cooper and Jane as his "driver and assistant."

Veronica said, "Buddy is like family."

Buddy shook their hands. He was soft-spoken and mannerly, with an accent Jane could not place. After Wolff insisted Buddy join them for a drink he sat and barely said a word. Jane sensed he was never at ease. He kept watching the door, observing all who entered. The waitress came and Buddy ordered an Amstel Light. When it arrived he never took a sip.

"Turquoise is a first-time starter," Wolff explained. "She's got exceptional pedigree, solid workouts, and if she can hit the board I plan on pointing her towards a race at Del Mar this summer. She's got speed, so if she can get a good post and a clean break from the gate she's got a chance. As a first-time starter, she should go off at a good price."

"Price? Your horse is for sale?" Jane asked.

"No, a good price at the windows."

"Windows?"

"Her odds," Cooper explained. "She should have good odds because she's unproven." And then to Wolff he said, "What do you expect the morning line to be?"

"At least fifteen to one."

All this was Greek to Jane.

"How much are we going to bet?" Veronica asked.

"Enough to make it interesting," Wolff replied with a wink.

Cooper proposed showing Wolff the diamonds in the morning before they set out for the races. "And if you're game," Cooper said, "after the races we could take a sunset cruise on my yacht."

Wolff seemed hesitant at first.

"Let's do it," Veronica urged.

"Alright. I'd like my friend Buddy to join us too," Wolff said.

"There's plenty of room," Cooper said. "The more the merrier."

"The races, then yachting," Veronica said. "It's a plan."

Jane saw that Buddy did not seem happy about the decision but he said nothing.

Walking back to their room Jane wanted to ask Cooper about his bloodstained cuff but decided to wait.

In their room, Jane kicked off her heels as Cooper removed his jacket. The blood had dried on his sleeve, now hardened and dark burgundy in color.

"What happened to your hand?"

"Nothing," he said and rolled up his sleeve. He went to the bathroom and ran water over his knuckles. "I told Jeremy I'd take care of the balance you owed," Cooper said before he dried his hands with a towel and went to the mini-bar.

"But we paid that," she said.

"He insisted on speaking with you. I explained that the people we were having dinner with can't know that you're an actress. He said that was ridiculous, and that both of us should be proud of our craft. I led him outside. I think he's jealous that we're together."

"But that doesn't make sense," she said.

"What do you mean?" Cooper said, pouring himself a scotch.

"Jeremy's gay. He wouldn't be jealous."

"No, not romantically jealous. Professionally."

He sat in the plush chair and kicked up his feet. Cooper used the ice-cold glass to soothe his wounded knuckles. "When he asked why we hadn't been to class, I told him you were studying with someone else. He demanded to know who it was. I don't know who's-who when it comes to acting coaches, so I refused to tell him and he became belligerent. He started back inside, claiming that *you* would certainly tell him. I had to stop him. Damage control."

"Weren't you afraid he'd call the police?"

"He was in no condition."

"But you weren't outside that long. What if he called the cops and pressed charges?"

"He won't," he said with quiet confidence.

"How do you know?"

"Because I told him not to."

This was a side of Cooper she'd never seen.

He continued, "Jeremy's got one big-ass ego. What does he care if you're studying with someone else? All he ever did was criticize you."

"I guess I let him," Jane said, removing her necklace, "and I came to expect it. Since my career was going nowhere, and I was so unhappy, I probably felt I deserved it."

Cooper joined her at the mirror. "Are you now?"

"What?"

"Unhappy? Because you shouldn't be. You did great tonight, thinking on your feet. You're a natural. I'm impressed."

He ran his hand along her snow-white slip and down the curve of her back, pressing against her.

Men had fought over her tonight, she thought. Cooper was the victor.

"Does it hurt?" she said, touching his hand.

"No."

She could smell the scotch on his breath and feel him getting hard. He kissed the top of her shoulder. Then he ravaged her neck, working his way down to her breast. The warmth and pleasure gave her goose-bumps.

He pushed her on top of the bedspread and went to work. It was rough sex, primal. Another part of him she'd never seen. For a moment she wondered if he was fantasizing about someone else.

Afterward, catching her breath as if the wind was knocked out of her, Jane was barely able to move. She dug out a turndown-service mint from underneath the pillow, unwrapped the chocolate and broke it in half. They shared the treat, kissing afterward, tasting the mint on each other's lips.

CHAPTER 18

Cooper got up before Jane to meet Wolff at the safe deposit box. She was sipping room service coffee when he returned from the bank.

"How'd it go?" she asked.

"As good as can be expected. Thank God he liked the real stones and we never got to the cubic zirconia."

"Think he'll take the bait?"

"Hard to say," he said then sized her up. "You're going to need a hat. Ladies at the track wear hats."

Jane pictured glamorous images of Southern belles at the Kentucky Derby in wide-brimmed hats. "Another piece of equipment?"

"Precisely."

They drove to a store in Beverly Hills. Jane liked the smell of the place—expensive leather. Cooper picked out a sundress and a hat to match. He shot down the sunglasses Jane picked out and instead went for an over-sized pair. Jane thought they were something an old lady would wear.

"These are for yentas. Forget it."

"Trust me on this."

"I'll look goofy."

"No second guessing."

Most of his decisions she agreed with but this one Jane was not so sure. She figured they could make the purchase but she didn't have to wear them.

Stepping from the Jaguar at Santa Anita Racetrack Jane's first impression was the art deco mural of running horses along the entire length of the massive grandstands. It evoked images of old-Hollywood, the era of men in fedoras and women in minks drinking cocktails and smoking. They made their way to the entrance. The crowd was mostly middle-aged men, many of them with the *Daily Racing Form* tucked under their arm.

They entered glass doors to the air-conditioned Turf Club and gave their names to an elderly woman at the counter. Jane noticed a sign requiring jackets for men. They pushed through turnstiles and rode an escalator into the grandstands. Jane felt silly because no other women were wearing hats. *Why did I listen to him?*

They were escorted past tables draped with tablecloths, napkins propped like miniature tents.

Wolff was standing as they approached. Veronica and a few others were seated at their table and Veronica was wearing a hat too, bigger than Jane's. *Thank God,* Jane thought. Buddy also sat near and greeted them with a nod.

"Thank you for coming," Wolff said, and hailed the waiter. Cooper ordered two Bloody Marys.

Jane sat next to Veronica.

"Alexander is a nervous wreck," Veronica confided. "I've seen him negotiate million dollar deals, ice in his veins. But horse racing somehow gets him crazy." Veronica then made introductions around the table. The others were apparently business associates of Wolff. They greeted Jane with polite smiles but were clearly more interested in chatting among themselves. It seemed Veronica was bored with them and glad to have Jane by her side.

Wolff refused to sit. Veronica begged him to relax but he paid no attention. When it was time Wolff escorted all to the paddock. He chatted with a man in a blue blazer, his trainer. Then a jockey arrived and mounted the impressive black horse. After all the thoroughbreds were led to the track the party returned to the Turf Club.

"I'm off to bet," Cooper said, money clip in hand.

"This is a tough field, and there's no guarantee," Wolff said to him.

"I believe in beginner's luck." Cooper marched off to the windows.

Less than twenty minutes later all watched the television monitor at their table as the horses were loaded into the starting gate. At first Turquoise protested going in, the track handlers having to walk her around to calm her down.

"Waiting on Turquoise," the track announcer said.

The tension at the table was thick. All eyes were on the television as the horse was finally loaded into the gate.

"The joy in life is anticipation," Wolff said aloud.

"That's poetic," Cooper said.

Wolff offered a smile.

"The flag is up," said the track announcer. The

starting bell sounded and they were off. The horses grouped together at first and then spread out on the backstretch. Jane had a hard time discerning where Turquoise was. When it became clear the filly was not up front. Jane felt bad. She wondered how much Cooper had bet.

When they rounded the turn the track announcer cried, "And here comes Turquoise, four wide!"

She could see the horse gaining ground, in contention, but definitely not with the leaders. But the horses surrounding Turquoise were tiring. The filly broke out of the pack and was closing in.

"Get up there!" Wolff shouted. "Go!"

"Turquoise with a sudden burst of speed," the announcer said.

Turquoise reached the lead horse and nosed past at the wire.

"Turquoise gets up to win!" the track announcer sounded.

Wolff threw his hands in the air. Everyone was patting him on the back, congratulating him. He placed his hand on Jane's shoulder, "See, you brought me luck."

Even Buddy came out of his shell, beaming, smiling, and waving his winning ticket in the air.

Finally Veronica grabbed Wolff's arm and pointed everyone towards the escalators.

"To the winner's circle," she said.

Jane followed until Cooper took her arm. "Not us," he whispered.

"Why not?"

"They take a picture."

"Right." She had seen winner's circle photos

before, in sports bars, friends and family beaming with pride. She wondered what Wolff and Veronica would think when they noticed that neither she nor Cooper were along for the crowning moment.

After everyone moved on she asked, "How much did you bet?"

"Nothing."

"Nothing? Why not?"

"Because only suckers bet on horses." He turned and moved back to their seats.

She took off her hat and followed.

CHAPTER 19

Jane's first thought was that Buddy was not properly dressed for boating because he wore his usual dark attire: black blazer and grey slacks. The outfit was appropriate in the hotel, nightclubs and restaurants they frequented, but awkward here. She wondered what kind of violence he'd be capable of if she or Cooper were to blow their cover. Would Buddy be the one to track them down? There was something about him that made Jane feel uneasy.

Veronica teased Buddy, commenting on his attire.

"Aren't you hot?" she said, the double meaning obvious, and more a statement than a question.

"Hot?" he asked playing along.

"You know what I mean. Aren't you warm in that jacket?" Veronica asked, trying to play innocent.

"Not really."

"You look hot," she said, playfully.

"I'm fine. Thank you."

Veronica leaned over to Jane and whispered, "He's afraid to take off his jacket in front of you guys because he carries a gun."

Buddy grinned and stared out at the water.

Jane had only the one pair of sunglasses, the ones Cooper bought her. Even though she hated them she put them on out of necessity. Veronica complimented them, but she still thought they were ugly.

The yacht set out and glided along the smooth water of the marina. Cooper pointed out the vessels owned by celebrities as Jane busied herself serving refreshments. Setting the sails, they moved beyond the breakers. Cooper handed the wheel over to Wolff who seemed to like the responsibility. Veronica found hats down below. She placed a captain's hat on Wolff and took a white sailor cap for herself, playfully snuggling up against him. Jane thought the cap worked on Veronica. The sun glistened off the water behind her—looked like she belonged in a Ralph Lauren ad.

It was clear Veronica had "sea legs," able to move around the deck with grace and ease. Sailing, skiing, and tennis were skills the privileged learned at a young age, Jane thought to herself. Kimberly would have these skills too.

"You're good on a boat," she said to Veronica.

"A regular Anne Bonny," Wolff said.

"Who's Anne Bonny?" Jane asked.

"A famous woman pirate seduced by the sea. Fearless, reckless and mysterious," Veronica explained.

Jane caught Wolff checking her out again. She smiled back, turned away and felt his gaze linger. It gave her the creeps. She wondered if Veronica had noticed—was pretty sure she had.

CHAPTER 20

Back at the hotel Cooper suggested they get a drink in the bar. Veronica claimed she was too tired, "Besides, I desperately need a shower."

Jane thought it would be best for Cooper and Wolff to talk business alone, so she said goodnight and headed for the room. She glanced back to see the men move into the bar. Buddy trailed them.

Jane took a hot shower, slipped into a robe and turned on the television. The TV offered the usual menu of the hotel's amenities. Out of curiosity Jane chose movies and clicked on the pay-per-view menu, then "adult entertainment." She curled up on the bedspread.

As if on cue a trailer for *Gemini* appeared but the picture had been re-titled as *Saturnalia*. Jane cringed at the image of herself in her revealing costume juxtaposed with the harshly lit orgy scenes, not part of the movie she'd signed on for, abstract enough to suggest she was engaging in these acts.

It made her so mad.

She went to Cooper's laptop computer and researched *Saturnalia*. Jane learned that Saturn was the Roman god of sowing and seeding. The feast of Saturnalia was a Roman celebration of the winter solstice. It was described by historians as a lavish orgy wherein slaves and masters switched places for the day. She searched numerous links until she found the porn movie *Saturnalia*, and a link to Zipper Video, the producer and distributor based in Chatsworth, California. Maybe she could sue them. She remembered signing a photo release and short-form contract but could not remember if she still had a copy or where it might be. Jane scanned Zipper's other movies, titles including *Sorority Sister Sodomy Soiree III* and one movie featuring obese performers in a historic New Orleans setting by the name of *Fat Tuesday*.

Jane hopped into bed and switched to an old black-and-white movie, *The Postman Always Rings Twice*, until Cooper returned an hour later.

"How'd it go?" she asked.

"Wolff is sniffing." He sat on the end of the bed. "Do you remember when I mentioned that this job may take certain sacrifices?"

"Yes."

"This is one of those times. Wolff has a certain request."

Jane jumped to her feet. "Forget it! No way!"

"Calm down."

"How could you even consider—?"

"It's not what you think."

"Yeah, well, I've seen the way Wolff looks at me. He's weird."

Cooper's tone became very businesslike. "What's important is that we close this deal. Don't you agree?"

Jane said nothing.

He took her by the arms. "We've come too far. We have to play into our mark's quirk and do whatever is necessary."

"What do you want me to do?" she asked, crossing her arms and pulling away.

"Wolff likes to watch."

"Watch what?"

"He likes to watch women."

"Who?" Then it became clear. "Veronica."

"I have a feeling they've done this kind of thing before."

Jane's mind raced. She remembered moments, in the spa or during evenings out, in which Veronica's touch lingered. Was she so naive that she hadn't picked up on it?

"How do you know Veronica wants to?" she asked.

"Wolff said so. It turns him on to watch her with other women. It's some kind of game with them."

"I won't do it. Forget it."

Cooper released her and walked away. "I can't force you. And I won't try." He sat at the desk and checked his email.

She could tell he was mad. A headache was coming on. "You're going to be pissed at me if I don't, right?"

"No," he said, but she didn't believe him.

CHAPTER 21

Jane tossed and turned, not able to sleep that night. Cooper was rolled to one side of the bed, snoring loudly, his back to her. She listened to the noises of the hotel; the plumbing knocking in the walls, a distant television somewhere. It seemed like such a long time ago when she first met Cooper, but it had only been a month or so. Her world was so different now.

Daylight was creeping through the curtains by the time she drifted off to sleep.

She woke to discover the drapes wide open, sunlight spilling across the tangled sheets. Cooper was gone. She dressed, put her hair up and headed for the hotel restaurant.

A waitress moved from table to table offering freshly squeezed tangerine juice and wedges of chilled cantaloupe. Another passed out complimentary newspapers. Jane chose a *USA Today*, not really what Kimberly would read, but Jane liked the pictures and concise stories. She thumbed to the entertainment section.

Minutes later Jane looked up to see Veronica crossing the lobby and waving at her. "Good morning," she said and sat down. A waitress approached and Veronica said she'd already eaten, would just have coffee.

"I slept late and I have no idea where Cooper went."

"I understand your husband spoke with you."

"Spoke with me?" Jane asked.

"About...us."

Jane leaned back, said nothing.

"I just want to say if you're not interested, I completely understand. I just hope it doesn't come between us. I mean, I've had such a great time with you, and I don't want you to think any less of me."

"No, I...If anything, I was sort of flattered, but it's just...not really my style."

"I understand," said Veronica just as the waitress appeared with her coffee. There was an awkward silence as the server poured.

After she left Veronica confessed, "Honestly, I don't really have that many friends."

Jane tried to imagine what Veronica's life was like, so different than hers. She seemed lonely.

"I really like hanging out with you," Jane said. "You're fun."

"I haven't been with that many women before," Veronica said, "but when Alexander suggested it, I thought to myself...Let's just say I trust you, so..."

At that moment Cooper, Wolff, and Buddy walked into the restaurant together, looking like old friends. They approached the table.

"Well, good morning," Cooper said.

"Where have you two been?" Jane asked.

"The bank for a little business," Cooper said.

"I was wondering," Wolff said as he took a seat, "are you an actress, by chance?"

There was an uneasy silence. Jane looked to

Cooper but his face was a mask. "What makes you think that?" Jane asked.

"I couldn't sleep last night, and I thought I saw you in a movie."

"What movie?"

Wolff shrugged. "You just look like someone. It's not important."

Jane could see Buddy was listening. Something told her Buddy had seen *Saturnalia* as well.

"He knows," Cooper said, back in their room. "He was asking me on the way to the bank, and I told him I was certain whoever he saw, it wasn't you. Obviously he didn't believe me."

Jane wanted to cry. "What should we do?"

"Deny it. He can't prove it's you," he said.

"What happened at the bank?"

"He seems interested, but I can't get him to commit. He's hesitating for some reason, and asking a lot of questions. I can't put my finger on it."

Jane asked, "Do you think it will help if I agree to be with Veronica?"

Cooper studied her without saying a word.

"Okay," she said. "I'll do it."

CHAPTER 22

Jane decided against wearing panties and slipped naked into a spaghetti-strap dress. Cooper buttoned the back. She put on her sexiest heels, kissed Cooper, and without saying a word left him in the room.

Under a full moon she made her way across the meticulous grounds to Wolff and Veronica's bungalow.

She passed Buddy sitting near the pool, reading a paperback under a garden light. He gave her a nod.

The door was cracked open. She entered, hesitant. The bed was neatly turned down. A bottle of champagne sat iced atop a chrome stand. She could hear the shower running.

"Veronica?" she called out.

"Just a second." The water shut off and Jane could hear the glass doors open and close. Jane wondered if Wolff was in the bathroom but then spotted him beyond the sheer drapes covering the French doors. He was out in the private courtyard and she could barely make out his silhouette behind the translucent veil. The wind blew the curtains. She could see the burning red cherry end of Wolff's cigar illuminated in the darkness. Jane turned away, went to the champagne and poured herself a glass.

Wolff coughed. She pretended not to hear it. As an actor she was trained to never break the fourth wall.

She'd finished her first glass and was pouring a second when Veronica emerged from the bathroom wearing only a black silk robe.

"Hi."

"Hey."

Jane resisted the urge to glance beyond the French doors.

Veronica crossed the room and stood beside Jane, pouring herself a flute. Jane could smell her shampoo.

"Pretend he doesn't exist," she whispered. "He'll stay right there and won't say a word, I promise. Are you nervous?"

"A little."

"Don't be."

Veronica put her hand on Jane's neck and caressed, then unbuttoned the back of the dress.

On the bed Veronica's skin was warm as if a fire burned deep within. Jane was embarrassed one moment, intoxicated the next, then back to feeling uneasy and even full of shame.

She found Veronica hypersensitive and easily aroused. Legs tangled. Hands explored. Lips caressed. Veronica may have been the most responsive lover Jane had ever been with.

Jane somehow knew what to do.

When Veronica reached orgasm Jane felt powerful. For a moment she was in control, and the feeling excited her. Then Veronica did her best to reciprocate. For the benefit of her audience, Jane feigned hers.

Afterward they held each other.

"You were fantastic," Veronica whispered softly and kissed her on the cheek.

Jane got up, pulled on the dress, found her high heels and decided to carry them. She crossed the hotel grounds barefoot, past the pool and was back in her room.

"Pour me a drink."

Jane took a hot shower and when she emerged Cooper handed her a glass of wine.

"Thank you." She sipped. "Perfect."

"How'd it go?"

"Good."

"What'd Wolff do?"

"I hardly saw him. He was watching from the patio."

Cooper seemed relieved. He kissed her on the forehead. Then the phone rang and he answered. After a few moment he said, "I'm glad you're aboard. We'll talk more tomorrow. Great."

He hung up, looked at her and said, "Whatever you did tonight...he's in."

CHAPTER 23

The next morning when Jane awoke, Cooper was already dressed and at the computer. He printed a picture of a streamline aluminum briefcase from a manufacturer's website and two plane tickets.

"I need you to take a cab to this luggage store and buy two of these suitcases," he said. "Make sure they're identical, same model, so you can't tell one from the other." He handed her six hundred-dollar bills. "When you return, have the valet bring them to our room. Don't risk Wolff or Veronica seeing you with them. Understand?"

"Okay," she said, and then glanced at the plane tickets.

"I'm going to switch cases on him," he explained. "We're booked to Tahiti on an open ticket. I need you to pack some of your things and put them in the Jag today, including your passport. Bring only a few changes of clothes and necessary toiletries. We've got to be able to pull out at a moment's notice. Got it?"

"Alright."

They ate a quick breakfast in their room. Jane packed a bag, including her toiletries, and put it in the Jaguar. Afterward she set out for the luggage store in a taxi.

Jane felt the driver's eyes on her in the rearview

mirror. They were pulling onto Santa Monica Boulevard when he finally spoke.

"You're clown lady, no?"

"Excuse me?"

"I pick you up before. You take off clown costume in my cab."

Jane recognized him. He was the same cabby that picked her up from the children's birthday party the night she met Cooper.

"No, I'm not from around here," she said.

"I never forget face. You undress in my cab. I take you to Hollywood. No?"

"You must have me mistaken for someone else."

There was an awkward moment until finally the man laughed. "Funny how some people look so much alike. You remind me of one of my customers."

They drove the rest of the way in silence.

Jane thought it best to not have the cab wait outside the luggage store. She tipped him well and thanked him. She could feel his eyes on her back as she moved to the store.

Inside she showed the print-out of the briefcase to the cheerful woman. She assured Jane they had plenty in stock. Jane purchased two briefcases, still in the cardboard boxes and asked the saleswoman if she could call a taxi.

A half an hour later Jane delivered the boxed cases to the hotel bellhop. Minutes later the staff brought them to her room.

Cooper returned. "We're in luck. Wolff claims he can come up with the money this afternoon. His bank offers a special service for its key account customers, large amounts of cash available immediately."

"Banks do that?" she asked.

"Beverly Hills banks do, ones with celebrity clients, or customers with business interests in Mexico or South America. In case of kidnappings they keep millions on hand in emergency reserve."

She wondered what a million dollars in cash looked like.

"An armored car is supposed to deliver it to his bungalow," he continued. "That's where we'll supposedly split up the diamonds."

"What do I do?"

"Keep Veronica occupied. Is your passport in the car?"

"Yes, I did everything."

"Good." Cooper began to pack.

Twenty minutes later the phone rang. It was Veronica. She wanted to talk about last night. Jane did not feel like seeing her, needed more time to digest what had happened between them, but Veronica was persistent. With Cooper coaching her silently, Jane agreed to meet.

"They have a wonderful tea in the lobby," Veronica suggested. "Alexander has some business this afternoon so we can meet there."

"A tea?"

Cooper nodded, urged her.

"Sounds good," she said.

Finger sandwiches, pastries and cookie-biscuits accompanied the civilized English convention of afternoon tea. Jane tried to mimic everything Veronica did and hoped her inexperience at such a thing wasn't too obvious.

Jane saw the Brinks armored car guards cross the lobby with a grey metal strongbox in tow. She pretended not to notice.

"I wanted to say that last night was extraordinary," Veronica said. "You were incredible."

"Thank you," Jane said, blushing. She studied the pattern of the china, an old English fox hunt, hand-painted and ornate. Men, horse and hound closed in on the elusive fox.

"I won't say another word," Veronica said, "because I can tell it makes you uncomfortable. It's just, I wanted you to know. It was special for me."

"I'm flattered."

Veronica lightened the tone and went into details about how Wolff had other kinky requests, some of them absurd. Jane laughed. Together they came to the conclusion that, deep down, men are pigs.

They made conversation with some other women at the afternoon tea, most of them grey-haired and elderly. All of them, it seemed, were guests of the hotel. Jane saw the Brinks crew return with their strongbox. She was dying to know what was happening with Cooper and Wolff.

Waiters served more delicacies. Little bits of decorative greens were arranged to perfection on every ornamental dish. Jane had never seen these kinds of cookies before and assumed they must be European.

When the other women were out of earshot

Veronica took a serious tone, confiding in Jane. "I also want you to know that, beyond Alexander, I really want to stay in contact with you. As friends."

Jane could tell Veronica was sincere but wondered aloud, "Beyond Alexander? What's that mean?"

"When he tires of me, or when our agreement ends. Whichever comes first."

"Agreement?"

"You don't get it, do you?"

"Get what?"

"Oh, I'm sorry," Veronica said with a condescending tone, as if Jane were a child. "I thought you knew."

"Knew what?"

Veronica leaned in and whispered, "Alexander is..." she paused, searching for the right words, "my client."

"Client?"

"I'm Alexander's girlfriend for now, because he can afford me."

The hotel concierge approached them, a thin young man. "Phone call for a Miss Van Cise. At the concierge desk," he said. Since Jane was not used to being called Miss Van Cise it took a second to figure out that he was talking to her.

"Excuse me," Jane said to Veronica, getting up, grateful for the interruption. She followed the man to his desk, wondering *Veronica is a call girl?* Jane couldn't believe it. She was too perfect, *too* beautiful. The concierge transferred the call from his desk to the house phone on the wall.

"I've distracted Wolff enough to make the

switch," Cooper said on the phone, "but he's holding me up and I can't seem to get past Buddy. Get the car. Take it to the airport. Park it at the international terminal and leave the keys in it. When I get the chance to duck out, I'll hop a cab and join you there. We'll meet in the airport bar, the one closest to our gate. Got that?"

"Yeah."

"Your ticket is in your name. Go now. Get away from Veronica."

"Okay."

"You alright?"

"Yes." She wanted to tell him what she just learned but figured it could wait. "Be careful," she said.

She hung up the phone then turned to see Jeremy Sands enter the hotel lobby followed by a man she did not recognize.

You've got to be kidding. She ducked behind a pillar.

Jeremy wore a neck brace and had a cast on his arm. They approached the man at the front desk. Jane spied as the man accompanying Jeremy displayed a police badge to the desk clerk. Jeremy had a photo and showed it to him. Jane could see they were looking at her acting eight by ten headshot.

The desk clerk nodded. He motioned to another clerk and they both studied the photo, even turning it over to scan Jane's resume on the back.

Jane thought about running but decided that it would only attract attention. She had to cross the lobby undetected, get outside and retrieve the car without Jeremy and the cops seeing her.

She glanced to Veronica who was still sitting, now thumbing through a magazine. Jane decided she would need to walk right past Jeremy and the cop, their backs to her at the counter. But then the men pivoted. They were walking her way.

Shit! Jane picked up the phone and pretended to dial.

The detective saw her. "Jane Innes?" he said.

Jane shot a desperate glance to Veronica. Veronica looked from the men and then back to Jane, confused.

"Jane!" Jeremy called out, limping beside the cop.

Jane turned on her heels. She briskly walked the other direction.

"Jane?" she could hear Jeremy calling out. "That you?"

She burst through the door and found herself in the kitchen. Steam and chaos reigned. Cooks shouted. Busboys clanged bus-tubs. She sidestepped a waiter and ran past. She almost lost a heel in the thick, wet rubber mat. Looking back, Jane saw Jeremy and the cop enter. They spotted her. Jeremy pointed, and they advanced.

Jane turned the bend and found herself at the walk-in freezer. A dead end. She could hear Jeremy calling her name again. The freezer was her last refuge. She decided to duck inside, but then got an idea.

Instead of entering, she hid behind the open door, outside the freezer. It was just like when she was hiding in her room as a little girl. None of her mom's crazy boyfriends ever looked behind her door.

She pressed herself up against the wall. The chrome door pressed cold against her face. She hoped they would walk past. Instead she could hear they stopped.

Her heart was pounding.

"Where'd she go?" she heard Jeremy say.

"Jane?" a voice called out. She assumed it was the detective. "Are you in there?"

She could hear the two of them push through the plastic transparent partition and enter into the freezer.

With a hard shove, she slammed the door. She placed the pin, dangling on a chain, into its hole of the latch-handle. She could hear muffled shouts from inside but they were barely audible compared to the noise of the bustling kitchen.

Success, Jane casually walked back the way she came.

"You cannot be here, lady!" a chef screamed.

"I'm leaving."

To avoid Veronica, Jane slipped out the side door near the restrooms. She circled the building and dug out the claim check plus a five-dollar tip. She handed the ticket to the valet, found cover behind a planted shrub and watched the door.

It seemed like an eternity.

Finally the Jaguar appeared and the valet hopped out. She handed him the ticket wrapped in the tip and got in. She took one last look back at the hotel before driving off.

She wondered how long Jeremy and the cops

would be locked inside the freezer. She laughed about how she outsmarted them. She imagined sitting in First Class, the plane lifting off, toasting with Cooper to their success, while Jeremy froze his ass off in the freezer.

Minutes later she was dropping down onto Sunset Boulevard on the way to the freeway. She thought about the bewildered look on Veronica's face as Jeremy and the cop came at her. She hoped Veronica didn't run to the bungalow, tell Wolff about it and spoil everything for Cooper. He did say he was on his way, didn't he? Maybe he managed to get away. There was so little time.

Traffic was heavy on Sunset. When she reached the 405 Freeway, the crack in the windshield caught the light—the skeleton hand reaching out at her, horrifying and freakish.

Jane took the freeway and got off at Century Boulevard heading for the airport. Her heart was racing. She wished she had a cell phone so she could call Cooper to make sure everything was okay. Once in the terminal she'd find a payphone.

More traffic near the historic restaurant at the airport with its retro-futuristic *Jetsons* design. She wondered how long it would be until she would see it again. This was the beginning of a new chapter in her life. No looking back.

Near the Bradley International terminal Jane pulled the Jaguar into the parking structure, as instructed, and found spot on the top level. She jotted down the parking space number figuring Cooper would need to pass this information on to the car leasing company. She took one last look at the chipped windshield, so ugly.

As she stepped out of the car, a pock-marked man approached her.

"Jane Innes?"

She stood frozen.

"Detective Myers, LAPD Robbery Homicide," he said.

She saw there were other men flanking him.

"Please open the trunk, ma'am."

"Why?"

"We need you to open the trunk," he said bluntly.

Trying to appear calm, Jane circled the car and put the key into the lock. She turned the latch the trunk sprung open.

Alexander Wolff lay dead inside, shot in the forehead, his tongue swollen and protruding.

He was staring at her, eyes bugged out, glaring.

Jane staggered and lost her balance.

The next sensation was hitting the concrete—an explosion of pain up her tailbone.

CHAPTER 24

"Like I could possibly have lice!" Jane screamed at them. She stood naked in the shower. There was a dispenser of foamy, pungent disinfectant on the wall.

"Everybody gotta delouse, princess," the female jailer said. To enforce the point the guard made sure Jane vigorously scrubbed her pubic hair.

Earlier during the interrogation at the police station she explained to them that she was the shill, an actress playing a role, but they kept asking about Wolff. She insisted the cops go to Marina Del Rey to track down Cooper's yacht. She told them her friend Carla would know all about it, or the gay couple Louis and Jim that had the boat in the next slip, but the detectives kept asking the same questions over and over. It was clear their only concern the murdered billionaire.

Jane realized she should ask for a lawyer. Once she made the request they stopped their questions, read her the Miranda Rights and booked her.

They took her to the Twin Towers Correctional Facility in downtown L.A. Jane thought it strange they would call a building the Twin Towers in this day and age, summoning images of 9/11.

Having surrendered her clothes before the shower, Jane was dressed in a bright orange jumpsuit, itchy and stiff from starch. The white, flat-soled shoes were too big and had Velcro straps instead of laces. She assumed no laces meant she couldn't hang herself.

They escorted her to what the guard called "K-ten Keep-away"—concrete-walled cells in a one hundred and eighty degree semi-circle. Each cell was visible from the jailer station in the center. Jane was told that since she was booked for murder she'd be partitioned here.

In the tiny cell she found the vinyl-cushion bed incredibly hard and the blanket was horrible, nothing like the Bel Air hotel's king-size luxury bed and goose-down comforter.

When she closed her eyes Jane could not shut out the image of Wolff's morbid death-face. It was like he wanted something from her—beckoning from hell.

Where was Cooper? Had he killed Wolff? What happened?

Some of the prisoners in the surrounding cells tried to engage her, a few spewing insults, but she ignored them.

She was allowed one phone call but she didn't have the phone number for her mother at Danny's garage. And she couldn't remember Danny's last name. So much had transpired since she'd driven out to see her mom. She could remember the racing insignia on his trailer, and that his garage was out of Sarasota, Florida. Instead she called her answering service hoping Cooper left a message. There was nothing. Next she called her neighbor Carla. She explained her predicament.

"I told you he was no good," Carla said.

"I know. I should have listened."

"The rat set you up to take the fall."

"You saw his boat," Jane said. "Do me a favor. Go to the marina. See if Cooper is there."

"And what if he is?"

"Then call the police."

"Okay."

"Thank you."

"You fell in love with a killer, girl."

"Tell me about it."

Carla promised to help, and Jane was grateful.

Only after lights out that night did Jane remember her mother's boyfriend last name was Dobson. Danny Dobson Racing, but it was too late. Lying on the bunk her throat ached and her head throbbed. She felt like she was coming down with the flu. To make matters worse, a woman's distant scream echoed in the darkness. The screams grew louder, pure madness boiling to the surface.

The next morning Jane conversed with the other inmates in the surrounding cells, even though she couldn't see them. Latisha was to her right and Kathy on her left. Neither seemed friendly, and Jane didn't answer when Latisha asked, "What they got you in here for?"

Breakfast was served on Styrofoam plates. The oatmeal was tasteless. The orange juice was undrinkable. The thought of yesterday's chilled cantaloupe and Kona coffee made it even worse.

She told a guard she'd remembered Danny's last name and wanted to make the phone call.

"Later," guard said and disappeared.

Throughout breakfast Latisha pestered with

questions. Jane said nothing so Latisha offered her own narrative. "They got me here 'cause the cops found my man's stash at my place," she confessed.

"That must have been one hell of a stash if they put you in county ward," Kathy called out from the other side.

"Yeah, well...it was the stash, and 'cause I gave my man the Ginsu."

"What Ginsu?"

"The Ginsu Knife, like on TV."

"You stabbed your man with a Ginsu?"

"Damn right. It wasn't no *real* Ginsu...Just a steak knife, but he got the point."

"I bet he did." Kathy laughed. Latisha joined her with a hearty, commiserating chuckle.

K-Ten Keep-away, Jane reminded herself. Probably best to remain silent.

After a while the jailer escorted her to the same room where she'd been processed the day before. Jane called information and found a listing for Danny Dobson Racing in Sarasota. She dialed that number but nobody picked up so she left a message.

"Someone here to see you," one of the jailers said, pointing to a pathetic man in his mid-thirties behind the partition. He carried a briefcase, wore a cheap suit, and his thinning hair was parted in a comb-over.

"Jane Innes?" he said, bad posture, shoulders hunched.

Something told Jane this was her public defender.

CHAPTER 25

"You're looking at capital murder," Paul said matter-of-factly.

Paul Nance was indeed the public defender assigned to her case. They sat opposite in the sterile room designated for confidential attorney/client jailhouse meetings.

"I didn't do it."

Paul said nothing and dug into his briefcase.

"Are you assigned a lot of cases?" Jane asked him.

"What do you mean?"

"Cases like mine. Do you have a lot of them?" Jane remembered from school that most public defenders are swamped with clients—spread thin and never able to spend much time on any single case.

"My share," he told her, glancing at his papers and wiping his nose with his sleeve. "Not many murder cases, though. You're my first."

She noticed his collars were stained brown, his jacket sleeves frayed, and his tie didn't match his shirt.

"But I went to Loyola with the Deputy District Attorney assigned to this case," Paul said producing a manila file. "So I've pulled a few strings and got an advance copy of the evidence they have against you. Our arraignment is Thursday. It doesn't look good."

"What doesn't look good?" Jane could smell cigarette smoke on him.

He pulled out a yellow legal pad, "Seems a .32-caliber pistol was found in Alexander Wolff's suite. Tool markings match the discharged shell casings. Coroner pulled .32 caliber slugs from Wolff's chest and those are in the lab now. Latent fingerprints on the pistol are being analyzed, presumably the murder weapon. The gun is registered in your name, purchased by you, only a few weeks ago."

"That's right. He forced me to buy it."

"Who?"

"Cooper."

"Who's Cooper?"

Jane explained how she'd met Cooper, how she fell in love with him, and how he convinced her to assist him in the intricate scam. Paul listened silently while taking notes, encouraging her to continue with little nods and affirmative grunts from time to time.

"A con man," he said.

"And I was the shill."

"There's more," he said going back to his briefcase. "Detectives are making inquiry into whether strands of hair found in Wolff's bed sheets belong to you. Forensics has requested both hair and saliva samples."

"Wouldn't they have changed the sheets?" she asked.

"There was no maid service that morning, before the body was discovered. A Do Not Disturb sign was on the door."

"It's my hair, and probably Veronica's too. I was there."

"In his bed?"

"Yes."

She could see Paul was taken aback. There was painful silence as Jane bit her lip.

"Interesting...in his bed?" he offered. "Please explain how that came to be."

Jane told him how she was coerced into sex with Veronica. She felt herself blushing as she told him. Although Paul was clearly uncomfortable, she could tell she had definitely piqued his interest.

When finished, Paul dropped his pen and leaned in. "You need to tell me everything," he said. "Is that understood? Keeping secrets from me will only hurt you in the long run. So please, help me help you. Helping me..." he said motioning to himself first and then pointing to her, "...helps you. Understand?"

"I'm sorry?" she muttered.

He shifted in his seat and continued, "A witness, the bodyguard Buddy Fahlderberg, claims he saw you coming out of Wolff's hotel room. Mr. Fahlderberg has been cooperating with the investigation. He says you seduced Alexander Wolff. He contends you two had sex before you killed him for his money."

"I didn't have sex with him, and I didn't kill him."

"Can you explain the missing three million dollars?"

"I was set up."

Paul rubbed his eyebrows, clearly distraught.

"You have to believe me. I didn't kill him."

"There's more. A man who claims he's your acting coach, a Jamie, uh...Jim..." Paul thumbed through his legal pad.

"Jeremy Sands," she said.

"That's him. He's a frequent customer at Heidi's in Beverly Hills."

"I saw him there."

"He claims you had him beaten up outside."

"Cooper did that."

"Jeremy spent two nights in the Cedars Sinai recovering but was able to track your whereabouts through limo service records.

"It was Cooper's idea, so Jeremy wouldn't blow our cover."

"The detective on the case accuses you of resisting arrest at the hotel and then locking him in a freezer."

"Yeah, I did that," she said.

"Another detail you chose not to tell me?" Paul produced another piece of paper. "The timeline suggests that's when you murdered Alexander Wolff."

"Do they actually think I had time to kill Wolff and place him in the trunk?"

Paul set the legal pad down and sized her up. "Do you know where Cooper is?" he asked, clicking his ballpoint pen for emphasis.

"No."

"If your fingerprints match the ones found on the weapon, and this other evidence stacks up, what makes you think a jury is going to believe you?"

"I swear to you I have no idea where Cooper is. I was set up!"

"Okay, okay...As I said, our arraignment is scheduled for Thursday. How do you wish to plead?"

"Plead?"

"Guilty or not guilty? I'm obligated to ask."

"Not guilty! I didn't do anything!" Jane said, trying to get him to look her in the eye. "You've got to believe me."

"Let's take a short break." Paul stood, fumbling in his pockets. "I can use a smoke."

She watched him go. Feeling vulnerable, all Jane wanted was her pillow, not the pillow from the hotel but rather the one from her apartment, the down pillow she put in the storage with the rest of her stuff. She wanted her old life back. She wanted to be a poor, out-of-work clown again.

Finally Paul returned, but this time with one of the men she recognized from her arrest—the pock-mark faced Detective Myers.

"Jane," Paul said, "Detective Myers and his team have a request."

"Miss Innes, can you identify Cooper's yacht?"

CHAPTER 26

After Detective Myers asked Jane to accompany them to Dana Point, Paul took her aside and said, "I don't think it's a good idea."

"Why not? I've got nothing to hide," she said.

"It's not necessary. If it is indeed Cooper's yacht they'll find another way to identify the boat. Besides, I'm due in court and can't be there with you."

"Tell them I'll do it," Jane said.

"As your attorney it's my recommendation that—"

"Tell them I'll do it."

She could see Paul was offended but didn't care.

"Jane, please..."

"Don't worry. I won't say anything to incriminate myself."

"This is complicated, and you don't understand the ramifications—"

"Tell them I'll do it."

Thirty minutes later Paul was gone and Detective Myers escorted Jane out of the jailhouse. For the trip they were accompanied by Deputy Sheriff Ling, a squat, no-nonsense Asian woman.

"Did my lawyer tell you about my arrangement?" Jane said.

"What arrangement?" Detective Myers asked.

"The deal I made."

Officer Ling hesitated with the handcuffs.

"A deal?"

"I get a good cup of coffee for the ride," Jane said, improvising. She never mentioned this to her attorney but figured she'd give it a shot. "Real stuff. Not gas station swill, but Starbucks."

Ling started in, "I don't think we have time for—"

"I'm not asking for a latte or espresso," Jane cut in, "just good, plain all-American drip. Dark roast. With a splash of milk."

It was a complete bluff but good coffee is one of the things she missed the most.

"That's not a problem," Detective Myers said. "Anything else?"

"That'll do."

Officer Ling continued cuffing Jane.

"I'll need my hands in front to drink it."

Detective Myers nodded his approval and Jane's hands were re-cuffed in front.

Emerging from the basement of the Twin Towers, the warm sun hit her face and Jane felt invigorated. Minutes later the vehicle was double-parked outside a Starbuck's near the Dorothy Chandler Pavilion. Myers went in for the coffee as Officer Ling waited with Jane, the motor running. The car radio squawked unintelligibly.

Myers returned with her coffee. Jane thanked him and took a sip through the white plastic cover. It was strong, like coffee was supposed to be. Although she knew the excursion would be brief, to be out of that horrible jail with a good cup of coffee warming her hands was heaven.

"I saw on TV," Jane said as they made their way onto the freeway, "that for every day that passes after a murder, the chance of finding the killer becomes more and more difficult. Is that true?"

"There's truth in that, yes," Detective Myers said.

"You think I did it, don't you?" she asked.

"You're a suspect," Detective Myers said. "My job is to simply gather evidence. It's the district attorney's job to build the case."

"What if this isn't Cooper's boat?"

"Then we'll continue to search for him."

Traffic became heavy. The longer this took the better. She wondered if she could get lunch out of the deal.

The cops made small talk. Ling said her daughter sold Girl Scout cookies to officers in the department and someone she called "Captain Crunch" bought twenty boxes, all peanut butter. That got a laugh from Myers. It was clear they were friends. Jane, the outsider, didn't get the inside joke.

As they drove she gazed out the window. She felt like a goldfish in a bowl, not part of the real world anymore, only able to watch it all pass her by. And like a goldfish, she was bright orange in her starchy prison wear.

The traffic lightened as they drove through industrial City of Commerce. By the time they reached Anaheim they were cruising briskly in the carpool lane. Jane craned her neck looking for the peak of Disneyland's famed Matterhorn ride but had no luck finding it.

As they exited the freeway and curved toward Dana Point Jane could see the ocean, sparkling in the distance. Myers made a call to the Orange County Sheriff's Department and told them to meet at the dock.

They turned off Pacific Coast Highway into the Dana Point Marina surrounded by steep ocean cliffs. They pulled into a parking lot and got out. Detective Myers produced a trench coat and draped it over her shoulders. She was grateful. The garment warmed her from the cool ocean breeze and cloaked the awful prison orange.

Momentarily a patrol car arrived. Two deputies got out and made introductions. One of the men was about Jane's age and completely bald. The other was older, African-American with graying temples who went to the trunk and retrieved a set of bolt-cutters.

A crusty dock tender emerged from a nearby office wearing a faded nautical cap and Bud Light T-shirt. He put out his cigarettes and led the way. As they approached the yacht Jane knew immediately.

"It's Cooper's boat," she said.

"You sure?"

"I'm certain."

The dock tender rolled portable steps over and the two Sheriffs boarded the yacht. Even though there was a padlock, the bald one knocked on the door and called out, "Sheriff's Department."

There was no answer. After a few more knocks they wedged the bolt-cutters in the door jam. With one yank it split the lock. They opened the hatch.

"Oh, God," the bald cop said, staggering back and covering his nose.

Myers stepped up to the door and peeked in before making a face. "We've got a bogie. Take Miss Innes back to the car," he said to Officer Ling.

"What's a bogie?" Jane asked, fearing the worst.

Myers did not answer and immediately got on his cell phone.

"What's a bogie?!" she repeated to Officer Ling as Jane was led back to the car. She was not given an answer and it made her mad. "What's going on?"

Moments later, sitting in the car, Jane saw the dock attendant stagger back, looking queasy. He took off his sailor cap, leaned over the railing and vomited. After wiping his mouth on his T-shirt sleeve he lit a cigarette and moved to his small office.

When a van marked Coroner arrived Jane was certain there was a dead body.

She witnessed the bald officer drape yellow crime scene tape across the gated entrance. More cops arrived. Coroner techs dressed in white pulled a gurney out of their van and stood by.

Finally Detective Myers appeared. He opened the car door. "Are you certain that's Cooper's boat?"

"Yes. Who's dead?"

"I'm hoping you can enlighten us," he said. "Game?"

"Of course."

"It's not going to be pleasant. We've got to wait on forensics, so this may take a while."

"Is it a man or a woman?" she asked.

Without answering he closed the car door and moved on about his business.

"Let me out of here!" she yelled. She hated being left in the dark. Who could be in there?

Later, the setting sun cast a golden hue across the water and seagulls floated above. Detective Myers reappeared.

"It's time," he said.

Jane got out of the car to see techs wheeling the gurney down the dock ramp. They wore masks and rubber gloves. A blue tarp was draped over the body.

Detective Myers reached down and pulled up some grass, letting it fall so he could determine which direction the blades descended.

"What are you doing?" she asked.

"We'll want to be upwind," he said, and escorted Jane to the opposite side of the railing.

The gurney stopped before them with a human shape under the tarp.

"She the one?" one of techs asked.

"Yeah."

They folded the plastic back.

Cooper's jaw was wide open, gums black. His face was puffed-out and eyes frozen in a perpetual glare.

She had to look away.

"It's Cooper," she said meekly.

"You sure?"

"Yes." Her heart pounded. Tears streamed. This was the man she loved.

Then she could smell the rotting flesh. It made her gag. She fell to her knees and vomited. All went blurry, the taste of coffee in her bile.

How could I have been so stupid?

She hated herself. She hated it all.

The second wave of vomit came. Then the painful dry heaves.

CHAPTER 27

Carla sat across the glass in the visitation room and said, "I went to the marina like you told me. The boat's not there."

"I know," Jane said. "It's in Dana Point. They found Cooper dead, and no sign of the money."

"He's dead?"

"Yeah."

Carla took that in. "I learned something more."

Jane studied her friend.

"Remember those two guys we met that night, coming out of the gate?"

"Louis and Jim."

"Yeah. I asked them how long the boat had been gone. They said only a couple of days, and then told me about a woman who used to come around, and another guy."

"What other guy?"

"I don't know. Someone other than Cooper. They didn't like this dude, thought he was an asshole. Didn't like her much either. I guess one day they got into it with them, some kind of conflict. They were shooting pictures on the dock. One of the guys is a model."

"Who?"

"Louis or Jim, I forget who. But they said this woman and this other guy got all up in their face about it."

"What was this other guy like?"

"I've got a picture."

"A picture?"

"They were super helpful, texted it to me so I printed it out at Walgreens. You can see them in the background." Carla held the photo up to the glass.

Jane recognized Veronica and Buddy, arm in arm, obviously lovers, cool and collected, masters of the universe. She had newfound clarity. "I think I figured it out," she said. "Veronica killed Cooper. She masterminded it all."

"What makes you so sure?"

"I didn't realize it until now, but it was Veronica we saw that night on Cooper's boat, the night we drove out to the marina. You saw her too."

"I remember."

"She, Buddy and Cooper planned this together from the very beginning. And then they killed Cooper so she didn't have to split the money," Jane said, devastated.

"Who's Buddy?"

"Wolff's bodyguard. Now it all makes sense."

"How?"

"Because she fucked me!"

Carla said nothing in return.

"And her performance was flawless," Jane said. "Perfect. I'm an actress. I ought to know."

The deception continues in

KILL THE SHILL

ACKNOWLEDGMENTS

To the fellow authors who helped me shape this narrative, I thank The Oxnardians (my writing group) including Jon Beggs, Bob Shayne, Roger Angle, Linda Burrows, Jamie Diamond, Patricia Smiley, Craig Faustus Buck, and Harley Jane Kozak. For inspiration and support, Jennifer Shepphird, Steve Jankowski, Doug Katz, John Hayes, Lawrence Maddox, Gary Phillips, and late pulp paperback author extraordinaire Tom Philbin. I also thank Roger Huyssen for creating such a fantastic book cover, and Eric Campbell for giving this narrative a second life.

ABOUT THE AUTHOR

John Shepphird is a Shamus Award winning author and writer/director of television films. He lives with his family in Southern California.

http://www.johnshepphird.com/home

OTHER TITLES FROM DOWN AND OUT BOOKS

See www.DownAndOutBooks.com for complete list

By Anonymous-9
Bite Hard

By J.L. Abramo
Catching Water in a Net
Clutching at Straws
Counting to Infinity
Gravesend
Chasing Charlie Chan
Circling the Runway

By Trey R. Barker
2,000 Miles to Open Road
Exit Blood
Death is Not Forever

By Richard Barre
The Innocents
Bearing Secrets
Christmas Stories
The Ghosts of Morning
Blackheart Highway
Burning Moon
Echo Bay
Lost

By Eric Beetner and
JB Kohl
Over Their Heads

By Eric Beetner and
Frank Scalise
The Backlist (*)

By Rob Brunet
Stinking Rich
By Dana Cameron (editor)
Murder at the Beach:
Bouchercon Anthology 2014

By Stacey Cochran
Eddie & Sunny

By Mark Coggins
No Hard Feelings (*)

By Tom Crowley
Vipers Tail
Murder in the Slaughterhouse

By Frank De Blase
Pine Box for a Pin-Up
Busted Valentines and Other
Dark Delights

By Les Edgerton
The Genuine, Imitation, Plastic
Kidnapping

By A.C. Frieden
Tranquility Denied
The Serpent's Game
The Pyongyang Option (*)

By Jack Getze
Big Numbers
Big Money
Big Mojo
Big Shoes (*)

(*)—Coming Soon

Made in the USA
Lexington, KY
04 October 2015